INTO THE WOODS

a dark fairytale retelling

KC ENDERS

INTO THE WOODS

a dark fairytale retelling

Print ISBN: 979-8-991 1880-3-6

For the lovers of fairy tales
...with a dark twist.

A Note

This is in no way a retelling. Though it might be considered a reimagining of a childhood classic that involves a boy, a bear, and a cast of familiar friends.

But now they're all grown up, involved with organized crime, drugs, and a hundred other terrible messes. For specific content warnings, please visit www.kcender swrites.com.

...oh bother...

Chapter 1

Devotion

Winnie

twelve years old

Sunlight streamed through the gently swaying leaves, dappling the forest floor in bright polka-dots that almost perfectly matched the bow swinging at the end of my braid. I'd salvaged the piece of ribbon from where one of my mama's friends tossed it toward the trash can. She'd missed of course, but that was just how things played out when Mama and her friends were celebrating. That's what they always called it when they got together and acted all silly.

When I was little, I had no reason to think it was

anything other than that, but as I grew older, I knew their parties were nothing more than an escape. That they were drowning their screams of suffering as the lives they thought they'd be living died tragic deaths worthy of Shakespeare, or one of the thrillers Christophe had told me about.

I didn't blame them for wanting an escape. Life in this town was shitty unless you were one of the elite families, and we had never been able to claim that title. But everyone needed a place where they could let their worries go, pretend nothing bad existed. A place where the world was nothing but sunshine and honey.

These woods were that place for me, but only for a few precious weeks of summer.

I shifted on the fallen log, anticipation making me restless and antsy. I'd woken up early, taken extra care twisting my blonde hair into a French braid—my newest skill—holding the intricate design together with the pretty scrap of ribbon.

I closed my eyes and concentrated, listening for any telltale sound that he was near.

We'd made plans yesterday, actual plans like a date. My first official date and it was with Christophe Robicheaux.

Every summer, for as long as I can remember, he appeared like a breath of fresh air and a hint of what the world outside of mine might hold. We were opposites in every way.

Christophe's family was rich. Mine was dirt poor.

Christophe's clothes were new and fashionable. Mine were old and dated.

Christophe's burnished hair was always freshly trimmed. My locks were unbleached and wild.

Christophe left at the end of every summer to spend another year at the private all-boys school he attended—the one he lived at that cost more money than I could even imagine. Living the charmed life as the only son of a wealthy family. Attending parties. Playing sports. Traveling over holidays and seeing the world.

My public school and peanut butter and honey sandwiches couldn't begin to compare to the lavishness of his life. But we were friends. Had been since he first sauntered into the woods that separated our worlds.

The snap of a stick had my eyes popping open and my heart stuttering in anticipation. Today was his last day before he left for another year. Would he ask me to be his girlfriend? Would he kiss me? My hands were sweat slicked, nervousness zinged through me as I checked to make sure my braid was still neatly in place.

As silence settled once again, I closed my eyes and tried to find calm with a deep breath. My hands on my belly, my shoulders rose as I breathed out through pursed lips, the honey-vanilla lip gloss that I splurged on at the dollar store mostly gone from the number of times my tongue had darted out in anticipation.

I was nervous.

I was excited.

I was ready and I was terrified.

"You waiting for me?" Christophe's voice came from nowhere. Without a sound, he was right in front of me. Closer than he had any right to be with as silently as he'd approached.

I blinked, taking in the boy standing in front of me, but just out of my reach. Leaves rustled, parting in the gentle breeze, casting Christophe in shadow.

As the leaves settled, he came into focus. Navy-blue shorts crisply pressed and topped with a bright white shirt, sleeves rolled to his elbows. Copper hair artfully pushed back from his face, stunning icy blue eyes dancing over me as he waited for me to respond.

Christophe Robicheaux was the most beautiful boy I'd ever seen. He took my breath away and stole the words from my lips without even trying. That part was new and had gotten more and more pronounced over the last summer or two—ever since my best friend at school and I started giggling over boys. She said I had a crush on Christophe, but I knew different.

"Cat got your tongue, Win?" he asked, dipping his

chin as he towered over me. There was a broad smile stretched across his face. Warm eyes and perfectly straight teeth thanks to the braces he'd worn in summers past.

With the way he'd grown so much taller than me and the way he was just so sure of himself, he was intimidating and comforting all at the same time.

A wave of shyness fell over me and it took so much more bravery than I'd ever known to squeak out a single word. "Yes."

He cocked his head to the side, his smile settling to one side as a lazy smirk played along his lips. His brows rose as he asked, "Yes, the cat has your tongue?"

I shook my head, eyes wide, lungs holding my breath hostage. "I was waiting for you," I whispered, my voice trembled, barely able to set the words free.

"Good," he said, extending his hand between us, palm up. An offer. A request. A silent demand that I gave in to without a single thought as I wiped the sweat from my hand and placed it in his.

He pulled me to standing, hands landing squarely on my shoulders. He held me in place, not giving an inch of space. His body crowded mine, his cologne crisp in my nose. He was so much taller than me, I had to tilt my head so far back, it hung between my shoulders, the end of my braid brushing low on my back.

"I like that—knowing you're waiting for me. What were you thinking about with your eyes closed and your face lifted to the sun like that?" His voice was deep and sure, any sign of the way it had cracked when we'd first met was gone. The hint of freshly shaved whiskers were barely a shadow against his pale, clear skin.

He was so out of my league.

So fancy.

So much older.

But, once again, he was here in our woods with me.

"I-I brought us a picnic," I offered, but he bit his lip and shook his head.

"Not what I asked. I want to know what you were thinking. What put that secret smile on your face? What had you pressing your hands against that pretty red shirt like you were trying to hold back a flock of butterflies?"

Each question held a hint of knowing, like he could see inside me. Like he already knew the thoughts skittering around my silly head. Like he was teasing me.

My cheeks flamed, hot and red.

Oh my God, did he know I wanted him to kiss me? Did he know how long I'd been in love with him? How many pages in the cheap spiral notebook I used as my journal were covered with hearts around his name and mine? How many times I'd practiced writing our names?

Winnie L'Ourson & Christophe Robicheaux.

Mr. & Mrs. Christophe Robicheaux.

Mrs. Winnie Robicheaux.

Every combination I could think of short of—

"Winifred, answer me," he demanded.

I flinched, hating my full name even as it spilled from his mouth.

I rolled my lips between my teeth, my own braces glinting in the sun, and blinked up at Christophe's raised brows and expectant expression. "I was...I, um, I was thinking about you and..."

"And what?"

A lone bead of sweat trickled down the center of my spine, my hands went damp, and my skin pulled tight everywhere. *Everywhere.*

"I was wondering whether you might"—I took a bracing breath and released it in a rush of words and nerves—"If you would maybe kiss me." I couldn't look him in the eyes. Didn't dare to glance up at him. Instead, I stared past his elbow focused on the tree that had become our unofficial meeting spot over the years.

Time stretched out, the silence expanded deafeningly as I waited for him to laugh out loud or step away, leaving me embarrassed and alone. I wanted to run. I wanted to take back the handful of words I'd foolishly spoken. Steal back my naive confession, and run home, but Christophe held me fast and firm.

As hard as I tried not to give in and look at him, the curiosity was too much for me to deny. My focus bounced from the tree to his shoulder. From his shoulder to the stray lock of hair that curled around the edge of his ear. When I was finally brave enough to meet his gaze, his brows were pinched together, pushing low over his eyes.

I didn't know what that look meant. Was he mad? Did he not want to kiss me?

Hope that had been buoying my courage started to deflate, cracking at the edges and crumbling to dust.

I twisted in his hold, my shoulders curving in on me, trying to make myself as small as I possibly could. If only I could melt away and disappear.

Then, in the space between one painful breath and the next, the woods spun around me and Christophe erased the small bit of space between us. He leaned in, like he was going to kiss me and make all of my dreams come true or tell me what a foolish little girl I was.

My heart raced in anticipation; my stomach churned as the butterflies turned to snakes tying themselves up in knots.

The closer he moved to me, the softer his eyes became. And when his warm breath hit my cheek, I panicked, afraid that I'd somehow missed the moment. I turned to face him as his lips connected low on my cheek

—but with the way I jerked, it was more like the corner of my mouth. My lips...

Christophe had kissed me. On. My. Lips.

He pressed his mouth to the edge of mine, his lips firm and soft at the same time. Like nothing I'd ever imagined.

I was stunned. Excited. Thrilled. But utterly shocked that he'd kissed me at all. And I was devastated that it was over way too soon. My fingers uncurled from where I'd had them fisted over my stomach, holding back the writhing serpents, and went straight to my mouth, as if I could capture his kiss and hold it there forever. The bubble of my crush—my first true love—expanding until it burst.

Christophe stepped back from me, surprise or maybe regret marring his perfect features. He shook his head as his eyes darted toward the picnic basket I'd brought with me. "I gotta go, Winn. I can't stay. But I didn't want to leave without saying goodbye." He took another step back, and then another putting more space between us.

Confused, I stuttered, sounding a little like my best friend, "W-w-what? W-why?"

He couldn't go, not yet. He was supposed to be here for another week. He never left me this early in the summer.

"It's for school. I have orientation for college before

classes start next week," he said as if it was a universal truth. Something that everyone got to do. But it wasn't. It was just another thing that separated us, one more experience that set his world apart from mine.

College was nothing more than a fairy tale for me. A pipe dream that would never become reality; it wasn't like it was important to my mom and dad. All they cared about was their bar and partying and their skeevy friends.

Bright blue eyes searched my face, a soft smile pulling at Christophe's lips—the ones that had just been on mine. His head canted to the side as he asked, "Was that your first kiss, Winifred L'Ourson?" His question was laced with a hint of something—teasing? Novelty, maybe? And when I didn't answer, but only pressed my fingers to my lips even harder, his mouth pulled up higher into a crooked smile. "I like that—being your first kiss. It makes this even more special," he said as he latched a silver chain around my wrist. The cool metal slid low, dragged down by a silver charm that was silently synonymous of our summers—a honeybee, fat and lazy, buzzing with perfect happiness.

"Be good for me, Winn." His thumb flicked at the honeybee and then pressed it gently where it rested against the tender skin at the inside of my wrist. "I'll be back before you know it," he promised.

Then he turned and disappeared through the trees.

As I pulled the tiny knife from my pocket and dug its point into the unmarred bark of the gnarled oak—our tree—it never crossed my mind that would be the last time I'd see Christophe Robicheaux for a very long time.

It was the first summer he left me early.

He was my first love.

My first kiss.

The first to break my heart.

Chapter 2

Death

Winnie

My focus is split between my parents and my best friend, Truie Cochonette. This isn't new, nor is the fact that Tru is going to win out, if you can call anything about this situation a win.

I drop the folded wad of cash I made in tips tonight into the pocket of my coat and turn my back on my parents.

"Tru, look at me," I say as soothingly as I can manage. "No, babe. Don't look at them, focus on me. Just look at me."

Her entire body trembles where she's perched on the landing of the stairs, her view into the cramped living room unfortunately perfect. I shift to the side in an attempt to block the scene behind me. Even as I die a little inside, the relief is undeniable.

This is the biggest loss I've experienced thus far.

It's certainly the most final, and if I were a normal twenty-two-year-old, I'd probably be falling apart just like Tru. Sadly, neither of us are anywhere close to being normal. We're both broken. Tru just a little bit more than me, and maybe irrevocably so, I don't know.

"How long have you been sitting here?" I gently place my hand on her knee, fully blocking her view of my mom's arm hanging over the side of the sofa. Lank blonde hair that only hints at a time when it shined like mine does nothing to obscure the needle still stuck in her vein, dirty rubber tubing coiled on the floor next to her.

I have no doubt that my father is in a similar state.

"Have you called the police?"

The question is rhetorical; there's no way Tru dialed 9-1-1, and not just because she's shaking like a chihuahua that's downed four shots of espresso. Not all cops are heroes, at least not the ones here—not the ones who found Tru, dragged her through hell and left her alone in the dark.

Her only response is a small shake of her head, one that if I'd not been fully focused on her, I would have missed with the way she's quivering. The outline of her is almost a blur.

"I have to call them, Tru. We need them to come in and take Mom and Dad away." Jesus, what are they going to do? What are they going to say? "Do you want to be here or—"

"I w-w-want to d-d-disappear," she whispers, anxiety causing her stutter to rack her body. Tears run down her cheeks like rivers overflowing their banks.

I stand, pulling her with me toward the back of the house. I hold her close, shielding her from the macabre scene in the living room.

Tru reaches for the door leading to her perceived safety, completely oblivious to the fact that she's barefoot and not at all dressed for the woods.

"Boots, Tru." I dig into the closet and grab a worn sweater in deep, dusky pink, wrapping her up in it. I frame her face between my palms. "I'll come get you when it's done, okay? When it's safe and they're all gone and..." My voice catches for the first time since walking through the front door after working a double shift at the diner. "And it's just us. Then we'll figure out what's next, okay? It's just us now, Tru, you hear me? We're free," I say, hoping the words are getting through her fog. Hoping she understands.

Darkness swallows her as she silently steals away from the end of our nightmare. We're finally free.

I turn back after closing and locking the door to get

the first, unfiltered look at how my parents chose to leave this world. And the simple answer is they did it in the only way that fit their lives. Expensively. Selfishly. And leaving behind a huge mess for me to clean up.

Disgust washes over me as I approach the room that for other families is the center of their home. Where they watch TV together, read books, share the happenings of their lives. Just not my fractured family.

As with my mother, a hypodermic needle hangs from my father's arm, the plunger depressed completely. Their faces are slack in death, lips tinged blue. Drool pools on his chest, staining his worn, dingey t-shirt. His wallet lays open on the coffee table in front of him, credit cards askew and completely devoid of cash.

Even in death, they left me with nothing.

I stare hard at their lifeless forms, digging deep, desperate for a tender moment that we shared, for a single happy, carefree memory as a family, but there's nothing. Not a damn thing. I lean against the fireplace mantle and catalog the waste laid out before me, and the only thing swirling through my mind is the massive pain in the ass it's going to be to plan their funerals. My gut tells me that the budget for their sendoff will be about what I have hidden away from waiting tables, and my escape from this town will happen a little later than I had hoped.

I turn my thoughts to Tru and pray she can hang on for a little longer. Just a little bit longer until I can save enough in tips to replace what it's going to cost me to plant my parents. That thought is almost enough to bring a tear to my eye, but I need *more*.

Never had a pet whose loss I can reach for to find the emotion necessary for this phone call, because relief is not what the world expects from me as I stare at my dead parents.

My only true friend is still with me, at least in the only way she can manage after all that she went through. The fact that Tru survived...

Distracted from my lack of emotive childhood memories, my fingers drift to my lips and though the charm bracelet broke a long, long time ago, the heavy silver honeybee remains, lashed to my wrist with a worn black leather lace, exactly where it was first placed.

A laugh erupts from me first, cold and hard. I was a foolish, love-struck child all those years ago, but the inkling of emotion, the hint of feeling is real. I close my eyes and let my heart drift back to the hope I felt then. The excitement, the way my pulse raced with that first kiss, with all the hopes and dreams and wants that filled me in that precious, naive, golden moment. The way it settled in me as I carved a rough heart into the bark of that tree, to stamp such a big emotion on the world in a physical way. One I could see and touch, visit as I waited for him to come back to me. One that ended up serving as a permanent reminder of what a fool I'd been. That I was discarded and left behind. That my childhood dreams would never come true. That as it turned out, the one person I'd thought I meant something to, who I'd thought saw me as something more than the rest of the world did, in fact did not.

A simple kiss, from a childhood crush, then I was cast aside and forgotten.

That's the thought that finally brings me to tears. I allow those innocent emotions past the armor around my heart and let them take me on a ride. I close my eyes and feel them, really feel them with everything I have, and everything I am. I allow the pain and heartache to amplify and grow and fully take control because I need them. I need the desperation of a first love, crushed and lost, to masque the relief I feel of finally being free.

Tears gather in my eyes, stinging and burning, until they fall down my cheeks in rivulets of remembered misery.

I cry.

I sob.

I mourn the boy I thought was different.

I mourn the fact that he wasn't. That I was just a game. A plaything to help him pass time sequestered out in the woods, away from his real life. The life I wasn't, and would never be, a part of.

When my throat is thick with it and my speech is sure to be muffled and broken, I place the call that sets the final chapter of this part of life in motion.

Hours pass before the commotion dies down and the house is clear, purples and pinks of the dawn of a new beginning leach into the dark night sky. Tru steals back in before the transition is complete.

"A-are you o-o-okay?" Her words barely register above a whisper, but the stuttering has eased. The stillness of the house and knowledge that, for now, all threats are gone seem to have settled her.

I lean in to where she's perched beside me on the creaky old porch swing and lay my head on her shoulder. For the moment, I allow her the illusion that she's taking care of me.

"I'm better than I have a right to be," I say, pulling a light throw blanket around both of us. "What about you?"

Her cheek gently shifts against the top of my head. "I'm…I'm okay." Just a pause, not a single stutter.

Thank God, because now comes the true test. I sigh but keep our connection and give her a pass on the funeral.

"You don't have to go, Tru. You don't have to be

there with me." I always give her an out—a choice so she knows she's got a say in what happens to her. Always. And honestly, the only reason I'm going to show up is because I have to. I have a part to play, a role to see through to the end in the charade that is my family.

"Y-yes, I d-d-do. You n-n-need me there. I'll...I'll b-be okay," she says carefully. "Y-you're all I h-h-have."

I tilt my head back to see grim determination on her face. The look is foreign on Tru. But I like it; strength looks good on her.

Twin caskets lower into the ground as the wind whips out of the woods, lifting my hair and swirling it around my face. The priest says his final prayer and I step forward, conjuring the tears that have become my shield over the past week. Each time I've reached for them for cover, they've come just a little bit easier. Practice makes perfect.

And now it's done. One more performance nearly completed and checked off my to-do list. One step closer to getting away from here.

No matter how hard I try, I feel nothing more than

relief at saying a final goodbye to my parents. Conventional wisdom says I should, but this whole situation—my whole life—has never even hinted at conventionality. Relief feels so much more genuine even as my façade of mourning stays firmly in place.

I drop a handful of dirt on top of each pristine casket and turn my thoughts to who their benefactor might be, because a double funeral does not just happen. These are the thoughts distracting me as people file past the pit offering their condolences. Who they are and how they're associated with my parents is beyond me, but I dab at manufactured tears that represent false emotions.

"Miss L'Ourson? I'm so sorry for your loss."

"Please accept my heartfelt sympathy."

"Honey, they are with the good Lord above, watching over you now and keeping you safe."

Again, that shit might be appropriate at a normal funeral, but not here. And the more people approach with their bullshit sentiments, the more I want to run. Escape and get the hell out of here.

I glance over my shoulder, scanning the cemetery as I shake yet another hand. The icy feeling of being watched prickles up my spine.

"W-we should g-g-go, Winn," Tru mumbles to me as she, too, scans the area. Her gaze pauses on a copse of trees at the edge of the clearing, stalling on a tall figure tucked among the shadows.

"Shit." Somehow, I think this has something to do with the financier of the pomp and fanfare and the pricey twin boxes hovering above a gaping hole in the wet earth.

Dark glasses flash with the tilt of the stranger's head, reflecting the meager rays of the sun, pulling my focus to a lone figure dressed all in black. The man is completely alone, hands casually tucked in the pockets of his crisp suit. Burnished hair styled perfectly back revealing a chiseled jaw and high, patrician cheekbones, full lips, and an aloofness that radiates out with authority.

Familiarity floats around him, hinting at recognition but dancing just out of reach in the blink of an eye. It's his sneer, though, that makes my blood chill. The cold dismissive twist of his mouth as the stranger stares directly at me.

"Who is that?" I ask, my gaze intent on him as he approaches.

Tru's voice trembles as she struggles to form her words. "C-c-can we j-j-just g-g-g..." Her nerves dig in and take hold, her renewed display of anxiety spearing me straight through the heart. It's telling that though she's evened out since the initial shock of stumbling down the stairs and finding my parents' dead bodies in the living room, all of her trauma is crashing down on her.

Years of therapy helped but at a time like this, anxiety just rolls over her, throwing her back to when things were bad. She slides her hand into mine, fear trembling through the connection.

"I don't know." Intentionally or not, I shift to the side, placing myself between my timid friend and the monster who is slowly approaching.

My heart stills and my breath freezes in my lungs. My hands curl around Tru's. What are the chances that my muse for the engineered tears this week would be standing in front of me? In a cemetery.

All I need now is a sappy soundtrack and for the spotty clouds overhead to get their act together and open up the taps.

"Winifred."

That's it. All he says is my name, but that's all it takes. The way his lips purse as he forms the syllables, curling at the start and pouting at the finish, has me frozen in place. My bravado is gone, leaving me nothing more than a scared baby animal caught in the sights of an apex predator in the dark and scary woods.

He stops in front of me, completely disregarding my personal bubble. Instead, he effectively dismisses the remaining mourners, tilts his head and glances around.

"You did well with your allotted budget. Bravo." Any question about who bought and paid for this circus dissipates.

I stare straight ahead, too rattled to meet his gaze. Instead, I note the strain of his crisp, white dress shirt as each of his measured breaths expands his chest beyond the shirt's ability to contain him.

"Look at me," he rumbles, his voice low and full of promises. The promise of something dark. Debts and dues. The promise of regret, though not his...certainly not his.

When I don't move, don't do as instructed, he reaches out, grasping my chin, and lifts my face to his. I resist, every muscle rigid, almost trembling, because I'm so damn tense.

"Winfred, I asked you to look at me. We can do this the easy way or the hard way, it's up to you. But I assure you, we will do it. We have a lot to discuss. Years to make up for." His dark, classic wayfarers shield his eyes, making him appear even more intimidating than he already is.

A tall, broad wall of muscle, steel, and torment. Because there is no mistaking the fact that Christophe Robicheaux looks like he's going to get great pleasure out of tormenting me.

Chapter 3

Denial

Christophe

twelve years old

"Go. Explore the woods and play. You're a child yet, Christophe, act like one. Get your hands dirty, build a fort, fight and slay the wild beasts of your imagination. Rescue the damsel in distress." *Maman* smiled softly and guided me toward the back door.

Far beyond the bright green lawn, gently sloping away from our summer home, was a forest dark and dense. The trees were so close together, they looked like a solid line separating this world from one that was completely foreign. Unknown.

Papa told me that it was important to know what was around me at all times. That I should never let my guard down and get caught by surprise. That I had to be the smartest man in the room. That someday, *Le Milieu* would be mine.

Maman still thought I was just a kid, but I knew our family was different from others, that sometimes they did things that others might think were bad.

I didn't know exactly what the *beaux voyous* did, but I knew we had bodyguards, and drivers, and didn't have to worry about how much this big new house cost us. *Papa* said it's always been ours, we just had to make sure everything was in place for us to be able to come spend our summers here.

That the timing was right, whatever that meant.

I stared at the thick line of trees; my hands shoved deep in the pockets of my shorts. "Are you sure it's okay for me to go out there alone?" The closest I'd ever gotten to that much nature was when my class at school went to special programs in the park for enrichment activities. Even then, we had my father's men with us and were never allowed to get dirty.

"Of course, Christo. I would never put you in harm's way." My mother playfully squeezed my biceps at the last two words. Her accent was still strong, very French, but she was always aware of how differently we spoke.

"Go now and discover a whole new world so you can tell me all about it over dinner tonight, *oui?*"

I nodded bravely, my chest expanding with the outward show. On the inside, though, I wasn't nearly as sure of myself.

One step led to many more as I pushed out the back door and crossed the huge perfect lawn. My friends from the city always returned to school in the fall full of stories about all the adventures they'd had over the summer vacation. Some went to their summer homes, some on months long trips to actual foreign countries, but they always had stories.

When I listened to the other boys brag about the boats they'd sailed on or the safaris they'd taken, I wanted to tell them about all the things I'd done, too. Except I'd had nothing to share. Museums weren't that exciting, not for summer break. Shopping and cooking lessons and French lessons and fencing were more like after-school activities, not summer fun.

I was protected. Sheltered.

This was different than anything I'd ever done, but how much fun would it be? I didn't have a brother or sister to play with, which was awesome most of the time, but right now, stepping into the cool shade of the woods, it might've been kind of okay to have one for company.

The air changed as I found a path between the trees

and stepped out of the blazing sun. It was quieter than I thought the world could be. Smelled cleaner, fresher than I knew was possible. And there was nothing to do.

I couldn't go back inside yet; *Maman* would be disappointed. More than that, she probably wouldn't let me. She wanted me to have an adventure, and this was where she thought I'd find one. I loved my mother, but she was crazy if she thought playing in the woods by myself was going to be a good time.

Sticks snapped beneath my feet as I wound my way deeper into the woods. I stuck to the path, because the last thing I wanted was to get lost out here. That might count as an adventure to my mother, but I couldn't believe for a minute that *Papa* or *Oncle* would be thrilled with that lack of attention to detail.

Uncle Alain was my father's twin brother—younger by a matter of minutes. Most of the time, Alain was angry. Didn't matter what was going on or how much fun everyone else was having, Alain was always pissed off.

I picked up a stick from the edge of the path and swung it at the trunk of a big tree. The crack echoed all around me as the stick splintered into a million pieces. I picked up another stick and swung again. And again.

When the last piece of wood hit the ground, and the air was silent again, a rustling on leaves from the other side of a fallen log had my head snapping to attention. I didn't move, barely breathed, waiting to see if I heard it again.

Being out there alone probably wasn't such a great idea.

The leaves stirred again, and there was a sound like an animal crying or something.

Cautiously, I peered around the tree completely caught off guard by the tumble of pale blonde curls just visible beyond the log. I stepped out and approached, slowly tightening my grip on the remnant of the stick in my hand.

There, sitting on the ground in a tight little ball, was a little girl clinging tightly to her right wrist. Blood seeped out between her fingers and dripped on the bottom of her faded red dress.

"Hey, are you okay?" I asked, rushing closer. It was a stupid question because she obviously wasn't.

At the sound of my voice, she startled and curled in tighter to herself, but she didn't make another sound. She went silent and small, clutching her bloody wrist close.

I kneeled down in front of her and put my hands out like she was a strange dog, and I was trying to show her I was safe. So dumb since this was a kid and not a dog. *Geez.*

"It's okay," I said. "I'm not going to hurt you. Can I see your boo-boo?" I rolled my eyes at the stupid baby word I'd used, but she was little, maybe it was good to talk to her in words she'd get.

She sniffled silently and with the smallest voice replied, "You already did," before shoving her arm toward me. When she moved her hand, I saw a dirty cut with pieces of stick and bark stuck in the drying blood.

My brows rose, and I asked, "That's 'cause of me?"

Her pitiful, teary nod tore at my heart. I'd never drawn blood before, never hurt someone even though *Oncle* told me it was time to start getting used to that kind of thing. My gaze darted around the small clearing looking for anything that might stick out, show that this was a test of his. There was nothing, but that was weird too.

I pulled my t-shirt over my head and cradled the little girl's wrist in it. "Are you lost?"

A sniffle and shake of her head was all I got.

"You out here alone?"

A nod.

"How far you live from here?" Maybe her house was close; it would make sense and then she could walk home and get her cut cleaned.

A shrug, a sniffle, and a tiny nod. *Great.*

"My name is Christophe; what's yours?" I rocked

back onto my toes and stood, helping her to her feet as well.

"Winnie," she said, smearing blood from her free hand across her face as she wiped at her tears.

Maman would cuff me good when she saw this poor little girl, but I couldn't just leave her here, hurt and bleeding. Not when it was my fault. My shoulders sagged as I realized I deserved the smack to the back of my head.

"How old are you, Winnie?" I held her gently but tried to steer her down the path toward my house.

She dug her heels in, not budging from her side of the log. "Five and...what's more than a half? I'm turning six next month."

Freaking hell, she was just a kid.

"Why don't you come to my house? My *maman* will clean this and feed you honey cookies for being brave. Then we'll get you home." It sounded like a good plan to me, but Winnie started shaking her head at the mention of going to my house.

"I can't. I'm not allowed to go past the log." Like she was making a point, she took a step back. "I can go home." She tugged at her wrist and grimaced. Sticks fragments and dried blood had pasted my t-shirt to her tender flesh and a fresh round of tears sprung to her eyes.

I followed her movement. "Wait...wait." I couldn't let her rip at the wound and the tears...her damn tears were too much for me. I grabbed my water bottle and pulled at the cap with my teeth. When it was open, I tilted it close to her wrist and waited for her to meet my eyes.

When her focus was on me, I said, "I gotta clean this and then I'll let you go, promise." I continued after she nodded agreement. "I need you to be brave, okay? It's just water, but it might sting a little. Can you do that for me?" I felt bad, because it was probably going to sting more than just a little.

"Uh-huh." Her lips smooshed together like she was determined not to show any cracks, but as I sprayed the water into her open cut, her chin wobbled and the corners of her mouth pulled down as her shoulders bounced with rapid little breaths.

I washed away the blood and the cotton of my shirt pulled away. Most of the debris pooled in my palm as she lifted her wrist from my grasp. With as much care as I could manage, I gently dabbed her arm dry, noting that the cut wasn't huge. Maybe it wouldn't scar if her mom put some salve on it. And a Band-Aid. And she really probably did need a cookie. Kids liked that kind of thing, right?

"Can I go home now?" she asked, fighting a tremble in her voice.

"That's what I promised. You want me to walk you home?" Why was she out here in the woods all alone? She was way too little.

"No, that's okay." She shook her head, eyes wide like she really didn't want me tagging along. "Thank you for taking care of me," she said and then turned and skipped away, picking her way along the path.

I watched her go until the trees swallowed her, and then I counted to ten. I stole after her as quietly as I could and caught up before long. I kept just enough distance that she'd never know I was there, but I couldn't let her walk through the woods alone, not when she was hurt. Not when she was so, so little.

We walked like that for almost half an hour before the trees fell away, opening up to the yard of an old, rundown farmhouse. It looked deserted so I stepped to the edge of the tree line, ready to follow her and bring her back home with me. Which, again, was dumb because I was just a kid, too. But even then, I knew it was wrong for Winnie to be traipsing around in the woods alone.

The screen door banged shut and angry voices drifted across the yard to me before the main door closed, cutting off anything further.

At least she was home safe.

Chapter 4

Debts

Christophe

Winifred L'Ourson.

Of all the fucking people I have to come down hard on, or take out and potentially unalive, it has to be Winnie. What are the fucking odds?

I haven't seen her in, Jesus, has it been ten years? A decade since I stole her first kiss and then turned and walked away, not knowing it was the last time I'd see her like that.

It *should* have been the last time I saw her, but it's not like I'd planned on...well, this. Though, I doubt she thought she'd be standing over her worthless parents' bodies at twenty-two, staring into the eyes of her worst nightmare, but here we fucking are.

Once upon a time, and a long fucking time ago, I thought I could save her, that I could steal her away and protect her. Give her something better, something akin to security. Thought maybe we could eventually be together and find a way to be happy. Thought I knew my place within my family. Thought I could make her mine and we'd ultimately rule *Le Milieu* together.

That pipe dream couldn't have been further from reality.

Instead, it's been a decade since I've gazed into Winnie's soft brown eyes, even longer since I've seen her friend. Not that the town's tragic psycho is seen walking around town on any given day. Nope, Tru has been hidden away and protected by Winnie for a long ass time. But I wasn't interested in where she was or what she was up to. I only kept tabs on Winnie.

"Winifred, tell me," I say, a bite in my voice. At one time, I may have had grandiose dreams involving her, but things have changed. I've changed. "Do you want it easy? Or should we do this hard?" I give her chin a quick shake to make sure I have her full attention. And I absolutely do. Her gasp quick and sharp, her lush lips slightly parted, the fluttering pulse beneath her pale, creamy skin all testify to that fact.

I like this look on her, pliant with maybe just a hint of fear.

The way her blush stains her cheeks.

The innocence she's exuding.

If I'm honest with myself, I don't give a shit what her answer is. When it comes to Winnie L'Ourson, I'll take what I'm due and fucking enjoy doing it.

"I...I don't know what you're asking for," she says, breathlessly, and my dick thickens at that sound. "I have nothing; my parents left me with nothing." Her sweet pink tongue darts out to swipe at her lips, leaving them glossy and glistening in the feeble sun.

I know she doesn't have the money to pay off Henri's debt.

Hell, I was the one who found him and his whore of a wife, pale and floating on their drugged up high, needles still stuck in their veins. Any fight they might have had was tamed, consumed by the drugs coursing through their systems. The same drugs they were supposed to be moving for me. The same fucking drugs they owed me money for. Rule number one of dealing is don't use the product. Follow the fucking rules and don't get hooked on that shit.

All they needed was a little extra push—literally on the plungers—and they were no longer a problem for me. Their daughter? She's a different story.

"I-I couldn't even pay for their funerals." Her cheeks flame brighter, more from anger than embarrassment at her admission if I had to guess, because we both know exactly who paid for today's circus. And I plan on collecting that debt, as well.

I keep my accounts current and clear, always. Aside from the expectation set higher up in the family, I pride myself on the fact that I keep my shit clean. Fucking crystal. Until Henri L'Ourson started getting sloppy. He knew he was in trouble when my second in command, Teague Grey, left L'Ourson's place empty-handed. No cash, no product—not that we maintain any kind of returns policy. That kind of disrespect is not something I've ever allowed.

Was I surprised Henri chose to take the easy way out? Not at all.

Was I surprised that he was so inept he didn't even complete *that* simple task? Fuck no.

I stared into his drug-glazed eyes and told him exactly how I would collect his debt, from whom, and then I tucked his offering of a small stack of cash into the breast pocket of my suit.

Henri was lucid enough to show fear, maybe even remorse for the mess he brought to his daughter's feet. But her mother was too far gone, had been for a long fucking time.

Then I pushed the plunger on each of their syringes, sending them off in a far kinder way than either of them deserved, and told Teague to take anything he could find of value.

There wasn't much. And now I have a debt to settle and a dangerous game to play.

"Your parents spun the wheel and lost, honeybee. And now someone's got to pay." The use of that nickname stills her, but only for a moment.

She tries to shake me off, swatting at my hand. The attempt does nothing but amuse me. Her drive and fire are cute, but the glint of a small medal charm lashed to her wrist with a worn leather band catches my eye. It's a honeybee, *my* honeybee. The charm I gave her in exchange for her first kiss.

"What do you have for me, Winnie? How are you going to pay your parents' debt?" I ask, sliding my thumb up to caress her bottom lip before I tug at the plump flesh. Goddamn, her perfect fucking mouth. I push my thumb between her lips, pulling her closer to me, shifting her off balance until her palms land solidly on the lapels of my signature Brioni suit jacket.

"Suck," I command, searching her face.

Cold.

Distant.

I remind myself that this is just another transaction, but deep down I know that's a lie. Nothing with Winnie could ever be boiled down to just a business deal; she's had my heart firmly in grasp since I found her in the woods that very first time. Doesn't mean I have to like it.

A thousand thoughts flit across her eyes in the matter of a heartbeat: anger, anxiety, interest. The only thing missing is desire.

Instead, I'm met with a touch of fear and a healthy dose of uncertainty before she finally gives and complies.

Fucking beautiful.

As her lips close around my thumb and her tongue hesitantly flicks at the tip, I twist my lips into a smirk. For the love of fucks, she is magnificent. Sweet and sultry, but all kinds of innocent girl next door. I could have so much fun playing with sweet little Winnie L'Ourson. Too bad she's supposed to be just a means to an end.

She releases my thumb, leaving a slash of bright red that matches her creamy lips rings my digit, and she scrapes her teeth along the calloused skin.

I fight hard to suppress the shiver that runs down my spine at that show of rebellion and strength. Yeah, I think I'm going to have a little bit of fun with her before I'm done with her. The fight for power will be hot as hell, and I could use the distraction.

"What happened to you? You were so...so..."

I huff a laugh. "You were a child; you had no concept of what I was then. This is who I've always been. I was born into this shit." I slide my hand to the back of her head, fingers twisting in her silky hair. I want to gather those golden locks into my fist and fuck those bee-stung lips until tears run down her face for real, because the tears glimmering in her eyes all day have been fake as fuck.

Even from a distance, I could see the way she fidgeted and shifted her weight, the way her gaze wandered during the service touching on everything but the shiny flower covered caskets holding the only family she had. Each time she glanced at her phone and sighed it was obviously from boredom. Winnie was not at all the mourning, devoted daughter and not a soul who knew the truth of the L'Ourson family would question that.

"You just saw a different version of me." I invade what's left of her personal bubble. "You got the watered down, politically correct version. Reality is much darker, scarier than the kid I was when I was with you. But this is it, Winnie. This is who I am. And I have a job to do, expectations now, that would make your head spin. And honeybee, you're caught up in the middle of it all.

"Now, you're going to have to pull up some of those fake tears you've had on the edge through this circus, and I'm going to console you and get us the fuck out of here so we can discuss the full situation, and how to get your debts cleared—"

She pushes against me, curling her fingers around my lapels. Whether it's her intent or not, she's putting on a pretty good show for the handful of others loitering over the grave. "They are not my debts. My parents—"

"Debts of the family, Winn. Consider it part of your inheritance. What was theirs is now yours and time is of the essence." I pull her close, tucking her face tight to my chest, until there's nothing but a breath of air between us. The scent of her perfume is intoxicating. Sweet and simple.

To anyone else, I'm sure this looks like nothing more than a tender moment—a heartfelt consolation of the grieved—but her proximity has my mind reeling. My head spinning.

I shake off the haze of her and lay out what's about to happen. "You're going to hold tight to me as we walk to my car. Then, when we're tucked safely in the backseat, we're going to discuss the terms of your repayment. Understand?"

Stress. Anxiety. Fear, or likely all of those combined have her standing rigid against me, her chest rises and falls with each shallow breath. And every single time she inhales and then lets that breath go, her tits brush against my suit jacket and I curse the layers between us.

"Do you understand me, Winnie?" I demand, allowing enough space for me to stare into her eyes.

Winnie reaches back and clings to Tru's hand, steadying the tremble as fear and anxiety push her timid little friend toward the brink, but her sanity is not my concern.

"Yes." The reply is small and almost as shaky as the hand she holds. "But Tru—she can't drive. I have to take care of her. We'll...we'll follow you."

I don't know if she actually believes the lie spilling from her lips, maybe she really intends to follow through, but my father didn't raise a fool.

Nope. And her friend is of no consequence to me right now.

"Teague," I bark, knowing he's close, waiting for orders. "Bring Winifred's car and her little friend to the house. Set Miss Cochonette up in a guest suite." I slide my hand into Winnie's coat pocket, extracting her car keys. I toss them to Teague and latch onto Winnie's wrist, tucking it securely around my elbow. "Miss L'Ourson will be coming with me."

For every step I take, Winnie rushes through three, practically jogging to keep up with me as I approach the blacked-out town car.

I wave off my driver and open the back door, guiding Winnie in and following closely behind.

"Home," I command sharply before hitting the button to raise the privacy screen. My driver may work for me, but he's owned by my uncle, and I don't doubt for a minute that anything of importance discussed in his presence will be reported to Alain Robicheaux at the first available opportunity. That's a lesson I learned the hard way. I paid for my mistake once, I don't plan on testing the veracity again.

"Christophe, please."

The tremor in Winnie's voice is delicious. I'm not a cruel man, considering my position within *Le Milieu*. But I'm unexpectedly enjoying everything about this little reunion.

"Not here," I say for her ears alone.

The remainder of the ride is silent. Tension simmers in the lush comfort of my car, shifting and amping up each time Winnie glances out the rear window. It's no mystery what she's looking for, or who.

"Where's—"

My hand darts out, fingers clenched around her throat as I cut off her question. "I said *not here*. I do not like having to repeat myself so not another word until I tell you. Understood?"

Her lips part, a response ready to tumble out. I turn and stare at her, my eyes narrowed, and even through the shield of my sunglasses Winnie gets the hint. She licks her lips and presses them closed, the bobbing of her throat as she swallows nervously slides against my palm.

Jesus fuck, it takes sheer will, pulling from deep down inside, to peel my fingers from her creamy skin. The rapidly fading handprint marking a necklace I can't wait to see on her again.

The house comes into view moments before the car comes to a stop. I don't bother waiting for the asshole up front to shift into park before I've got the door open and am dragging Winnie out with me. I need to make sure we're alone before she opens her goddamn mouth, because if I have to shut her up again, I might be tempted to shove my dick in her mouth. Fucking plump red lips would look hot as shit wrapped around my favorite appendage.

Chapter 5

Due

Winnie

I stumble after Christophe, barely escaping a full face plant on the gravel of the drive only because he catches me. Not a sweet, romantic catch, but utilitarian and efficient. Utterly powerful and in control.

My head is spinning with everything that is happening today.

It was supposed to be a simple burial. That's all I had on my to-do list today—that's it. But my entire day has been flipped upside down and somehow, I ended up being kidnapped. Because there is no doubt in my mind that's exactly what this is. I'm here, at what has to be his house, for the first time ever and it's entirely against my will.

Christophe drags me up the gray stone steps flanked on either side by concrete lions, through a massive dark wood door and into his house.

Silence hangs between us for as long as I can stand it, and then all of my simmering questions come tumbling free.

"Where are we? What...what are you doing to Tru? Where is she?"

Concern for my friend's safety battles hard with my concern for her current state of mind. She's...delicate. Damaged and lost in the darkness of the demons that have haunted her since before she was taken.

Maybe it's foolish of me not to be more concerned for myself, because I'm obviously in some deep shit here.

Foolish of me, but I'm also more than a little bit intrigued. I don't even know how much there is to unpack from this whole experience, but now is not the time to figure that out.

I can handle this—whatever *this* is.

"Teague's taking care of her. She's fine," he says, tilting his head in my direction.

My cheeks flush, definitely in anger this time, and a small muscle in my jaw jumps as I clench my teeth and turn, straining to look out the window at the long driveway disappearing into the trees.

"Where? Her safety, her security is being with me," I

inform him. "They turned. Why didn't they follow us? Where is he taking her?" Panic leaches into my voice.

"They're coming here, to my house—eventually. Miss Cochonette will have her own private suite and will be well attended. I assure you, she is fine."

"But—"

He pulls the sunglasses from his face and tosses them on the table in the center of the foyer. The clatter draws my attention back inside.

Dark wood bathes the walls in moody light and masculinity. Dark floors are covered in even darker rugs, the whole thing screams villainous hideaway or the devil's lair.

I should be scared.

I should be shaking in my cheap thrift-store shoes.

Honestly, I should be shitting my pants.

He narrows his eyes at me. "And we don't want an audience while we discuss your current situation. Your first installment is due immediately."

He turns and stalks into the room to the left of the foyer and if I thought the entryway was dark and moody, this room is downright intimidating. It feels like the kind of room scary deals are made in, murders plotted, and the coverup tasks assigned. Like maybe I should be looking for a roll of plastic sheeting tucked into a corner to wrap up the bodies of a meeting gone bad.

Christophe reaches for a whiskey decanter and splashes some of the amber liquid into a cut crystal tumbler.

"Installment?" I ask warily.

"Your debt. It has to be paid." He lifts the glass to his mouth and the whisper of a memory tingles at the edge of my mind.

Once upon a time, those lips were pressed against mine. It was chaste, nothing more than an innocent brush, but it was a kiss that I stole. The memory of which I manipulated and twisted in my mind to make it something more.

I was young back then. I was definitely foolish, but I was just a child playing at a game I had no business messing with. It was a lot of years ago, almost a lifetime.

I'm not sure much has changed. Now, I'm in way over my head with this new version of Christophe. Because this game, his business, and the reasons my parents were in his debt are, without a doubt, no good.

My mind whirs with thoughts and ideas on how to navigate this, but the problems are packed in tight like a dense forest that won't allow for even a single ray of sunlight to filter through to the ground. The whole thing feels impossibly hopeless.

I release a breath, praying that the tremor of nerves is hidden yet knowing full well that it's there for the world to see. Not the world, Christophe. Nothing escaped his notice when we were kids, I don't know why I think that might have changed.

"My purse is in my car. As soon as your friend gets here with Tru, I'll give you everything I have. It's not much, but it's yours. And my job—you can have my paycheck, my tips, all of it. I just need enough to feed Tru and me. And a little for gas, the house is paid off."

It's doable. My escape from this town will just take a little bit longer to come to fruition, but I've survived this long. A few more months—a year—won't make that big of a difference. And then we'll be free.

A dark chuckle pulls me back from my errant thoughts.

"That's not going to work."

"What do you mean it's not going to work?" I throw my hands out to either side, incredulous. "It's money. I'll give you as much as I can until the stupid debt is paid in full. However long that takes."

Christophe turns to face me, leaning back against the edge of his desk, feet crossed at the ankles. "What kind of money do you think we're talking about here? What do you do, make lattes and frappés? Wait tables?"

I shift my weight, my hip popping and attitude rising. When I notice his lifted brow, I stand straight again, ignoring the pinch of my toes in the higher-than-normal stilettos I'm wearing. I'm more of a cute boots and sneakers kind of girl, but you know, funerals and all.

"There is nothing wrong with waiting tables." My retort falls flat in the expansive study. It's so big, there would be an echo if not for the thick rugs and plush furnishings scattered about the space.

"With interest, you'd never get your head above water," he says simply. "Tens of thousands, Winnie. Compounding daily. Think big. And that's not even taking into account the greater issue."

Holy shit, this is bad. Really bad. "Why? What..." I let the question fade into nothingness, because I know. Deep down, I've always known that my parents used drugs. Eventually, I knew they had a serious problem. Parties, empty pantry, missed school events. Even as a child, I knew there was more than forgetfulness to blame for their shortcomings. "The house. You can have their house. That should cover what they owe, right? And the club. I don't want anything to do with that place." The tension in my shoulders eases at the prospect.

"Seriously?"

"Absolutely. Take them both and we'll call this good." Relief is short-lived.

"I own both the house and their business outright," he says coolly. "What else have you got for me?"

I'm dumbfounded.

I had no idea about...well...any of this. Holy shit, what am I going to do? My gaze darts around the room, looking for an escape, a way out that just doesn't seem to exist.

"I have nothing." Not a fucking thing to my name. Hell, I'm actually homeless now, because I can't go back to the house I grew up in knowing it's really his.

"Surely you can think of something you have that someone might find of value." He rakes his gaze down my body, caressing every inch of me, every curve, before reversing the route and meeting the panic in my eyes.

"Nothing. I don't have anything to give you," I say again. There's really no way out of this. I'm stuck. Even in death, my parents have fucked me over.

His head tilts and dips to the side, almost coy, like he knows something I don't. Which, let's be honest, I feel like I'm three steps behind him and falling further back the longer this conversation goes on.

"Come here," he says, taking another sip from his glass.

I take a tentative step forward.

"Closer."

Another step.

"Jesus fucking Christ, Winifred. Come. To. Me."

I flinch, not just at his tone, though that's enough to

send a shiver down my spine, but the use of my full name again. I hate it.

"I hate everything about that name," I say. "You never used to call me that." My voice is small. Weak. Bumbling. "You used to call me Winn when we were kids. What happened to you?"

He huffs a laugh, but it's not a happy one. This laugh is sad. Angry. Full of nothing but discontent.

"More than you can imagine. You wouldn't believe the shit I've been through since I last saw you in the woods," he says. "But I was never a kid, Winnie—not really. I wasn't allowed the luxury of having a real childhood. Any freedom I knew, any carefree moments, all happened in those woods with a little girl who had the sweetest disposition and honey-blonde braids. Your innocence is the only thing I ever experienced that hinted at what a childhood was supposed to be. You and those goddamn woods were my escape from the shitstorm of my reality."

My head snaps back like I've been slapped. "You think you had a shit childhood? You're kidding me, right? How many times did you get shoved out of the house so you didn't disturb your parents' parties? How many times did you stuff your feet into shoes that were torn and two sizes too small? Did you ever go to bed hungry?" An angry laugh huffs free as flames of embarrassment crawl up my neck, heating my cheeks. "Tell me...how many times did you run to your room, looking for an escape, a safe place to lock yourself away, only to find a stranger passed out on your bed? Or better yet, fucking on it? Huh? How many times, Christophe?"

Memories flood back in of all the times I escaped from that fucked up life, running through the woods. Curling up with a threadbare blanket under our tree, praying that Christophe would be there. Knowing that, even in the summer, there was no way he would know to come, that he never knew how much I needed those few precious weeks each summer to pretend that my life was okay.

Tears sting at my eyes, threatening to fall. It's sheer will that keeps them from spilling and trailing down my face. Years and years of neglect and need instilled a stubborn streak in me that is still a mile wide. And if this is a dick measuring contest with Christophe Robicheaux, it's one I'm going to win.

Emotion swirls in his eyes—anger maybe, or remorse —before they go cold and hard again. Nothing like not addressing the elephant, not even hiding in plain sight. No, this one is sitting right in the middle of everything in a hot pink tutu with streamers raining down on it.

He pushes off the desk and obliterates the space between us, much like he did the last time I saw him.

Only then, he really was smiling. Now though, it seems like the world is pressing down on him, a black cloud just over his shoulder casting him in ominous shadow.

He's so close I can feel him brush against me with each inhaled breath. His broad, muscled chest grazing against me has my core tightening and my nipples drawing into tight peaks.

He lifts the glass of whiskey and drains half the contents all while keeping me captive in his steely stare. The intensity of his ice-blue eyes is almost overwhelming. I should be shaking in my wannabe Louboutins. The only reason I'm not, is because I didn't want to waste the money on red paint to cover the soles of my cheap shoes. Make no mistake, though, I am absolutely shaking.

Nerves. Excitement. Anticipation.

Unexpected thoughts race through my head, spinning and whirling until my brain is a muddled, sticky pile of goo.

Why is he so close?

Is he going to kiss me?

Do I want him to?

The last question is the only one I can answer and that is a resounding yes. The jolt of that realization is enough to make me jerk away from Christophe. And as much as that doesn't make a lick of sense, his reaction to my move is...everything.

His free hand darts out and he cups the back of my head, holding me in place. My scalp stings, dancing on the edge of pain as he weaves his fingers through my hair, locking my tresses in his fist.

I can't move.

I don't want to.

I want to live here, in the dark and shadows of this moment, breathing in this man. His scent of sandalwood and whiskey. His confidence. The danger and intrigue that swirl around him in a haze so thick, it wraps around us like mist in the woods.

My first crush.

The last person I thought I'd ever see again.

Chapter 6

Danger

Winnie

ten years old

I DRAGGED MY FEET, DOING EVERYTHING I COULD TO delay going home. Every other kid I knew was celebrating the last day of the school year. I was dreading the loss of my sanctuary.

During the school year, I knew I'd get fed at least once on any given weekday; real food, not just crap from the gas station near my parents' club. I knew I'd be safe for the entire day, with no one passed out drunk or shooting up drugs in the bathroom. I knew that someone gave a shit that I was okay, even if it was just a handful of hours.

Someone cared. Someone wanted me to learn, to succeed. To become something *more*.

The only time I felt any of that outside of school was in the couple of weeks toward the end of each summer, when Christophe would show up in the woods. Meeting him at our tree as the July heat rolled into August was the one thing I looked forward to once that final school bell rang in the spring.

I hated the time in between.

Most of the kids in town spent their summer vacations traveling with their families, visiting the beach, hiking in the mountains, spending weeks at summer camps, or hanging out with their cousins at their grandparents' house.

Even my best friend, Tru, left. Her parents were divorced, and her mom lived hours away. Tru spent the school year living with her father, but holidays and summers she was always with her mom. I think the arrangement was easier on them, but something about it made Tru nervous. Each time she left for her mom's house she was happy, carefree aside from telling me how much she was going to miss me and how she wished she could take me with her.

She wasn't alone in that; I wished I could go with

her too, at least for the bulk of the summer. I didn't ever want to miss out on the time that Christophe was here. That time was special.

But within a few days of being back in town with her dad, she changed. Tru grew quieter again, keeping mostly to herself with me as her only real friend.

I loved Tru like she was my sister. If I was never going to have a real sister, there was no one else I'd rather pick than Tru. I didn't get an allowance, heck, there were a lot of things I didn't get that other kids did, but I found beads scattered across the floor of my bedroom last time my mama had her friends over. I gathered them up and strung them together on some thread and made special bracelets for me and Tru—friendship bracelets.

The other kids in school made fun of us. Called us names and always found ways to keep us at a distance. But we had each other and that was all that mattered. Except when she left...

I walked as slowly as I could, took the long way home, but there was no avoiding it anymore. It was hot out and I was thirsty. If I was lucky, I might only have an hour or two until Mama had to leave to meet my dad at their club.

When I was littler, I got scared when they left me home alone at night. Now that I was older, being alone was a relief. I could lock the doors and turn out all the lights, make sure none of their friends thought anyone was there. I could hide. Curl up in my bed with a flashlight and the new book my teacher gave me. She said it was for my summer reading assignment, but I don't know.

Sometimes when things were really bad over the long break from school, things showed up at my house. Stuff that was just for me. Usually it was food, healthy snacks and the most amazing honey cookies. Those only came rarely and almost always late enough in the summer so I made sure to save some and share them with Christophe. Though maybe he didn't like the cookies; he never ate more than a half and that was only when I insisted. I loved those cookies.

I crept up the stairs to the back of the house, toeing off my beat-up sneakers and tucking them into the coat closet. The house was quiet, but that didn't necessarily mean that I was alone, that it was safe.

Nothing seemed out of place, no one sprawled on the sofa as I made my way through the living room, but whatever false hope I'd had that I might be alone, was dashed as my foot hit the landing of the stairs.

A man loomed at the top of the staircase. He wasn't anyone I knew, and as I watched him adjust the leather straps around his shoulder, a chill skated down my spine.

The glint of polished steel tucked in the holster had me retreating until my back hit the wall.

Black, greasy hair was slicked straight back from his face, a mustache that was so thin it looked drawn in place accented the lift of his lip as he stared at me. He started down the steps, one by one, as he tucked his barely buttoned shirt into shiny silver-gray dress pants.

"What do we have here?" he asked.

I didn't know if he was addressing me, but my words stuck in my throat as I trembled. There were three steps to my right that would take me back down to the living room, but I was frozen in place.

"Cormac? Who're you talking to?" my mother slurred. She pulled a flimsy robe around her, securing the sash at her waist as she got to the top of the stairs. "Why you leaving already, baby? Thought you could last longer than that, didn't even get to come."

She didn't look at me or acknowledge that I was there and maybe that was a gift from God himself, because the man stopped halfway down the stairs and turned toward her.

I shook off what I could of the ice that had frozen in my veins and inched to the right. I was one of the fastest runners in my P.E. class at school, but I didn't think I could outrun a full-grown man. Whatever head start I could manage was literally going to be the difference between life and death.

"The fuck you talking about, Claudette, huh? Whores don't get to come. Shut your fucking mouth and—"

I didn't hear the rest of what he said. With a burst of adrenaline fueled fear, I threw myself down the short set of steps and flung myself through the house and right back out the door I'd just come in. I hadn't spared time to grab my shoes or anything for that matter, I just ran.

Rocks and twigs and forest debris pricked at the bottoms of my feet as I ran as if my life depended on it into the woods. And somewhere in the pit of my stomach, I was pretty sure it did.

I wound my way through the trees, hiding periodically to see if that man, Cormac, was following me. When it was clear that he didn't, or at least didn't long enough to make a difference, I snuck through the shaded woods to my tree.

It could have been minutes that I sat there, it was definitely more like hours. When the sun went down and the evening chill swept into the evening, I tucked myself against the bark of the fallen log and closed my eyes.

I didn't think about small woodland animals that were likely scurrying along the ground looking for shelter or food. I didn't care that I was completely exposed. The thought of dying in the woods was so much better than whatever might have happened back at my house, that much I knew.

That summer, I spent a lot of nights sleeping in the woods, surrounded by night sounds, knowing that I would see Christophe every morning, as soon as he was able to get away.

Chapter 7

Deals

Christophe

Sunshine, innocence, and pure sweetness, that's what she is. Her eyes widen with surprise as I grip her hair, her lips parting in a silent gasp.

The draw is strong.

She is temptation and sin wrapped in cheap clothing and desperation.

And I need a taste. Just one little taste to see if she's still as sweet as I remember.

I lean in and press my mouth to hers, to the same spot I kissed her all those years ago. When she was nothing more than a child and I thought I still had a lifetime ahead of me.

How wrong I was.

Her eyes drift closed as she tilts her head, granting me access. Giving me more. Soft full lips that taste sweet like honey. Allowing me to explore her mouth and lose myself in everything that was before. Before I walked away from the naïve child in the woods and entered hell on earth.

I can't do this.

I can't allow myself to fall into the fantasy of what could have been if I hadn't snuck off to entertain the kid who'd had an innocent crush on me.

She was practically a baby.

I was almost a man.

Puppy love. That's what *Maman* called it. She'd told me to let the girl down gently and say goodbye before stepping into my role within *Le Milieu*.

That was the last thing we talked about. Winnie and her crush.

Anger rolls through me and I can feel Winnie tense against me. She tries to pull back and the whimper, that sweet little whine of fear when I don't release her, has the unexpected result of making my dick swell. I can't get wrapped up in this—in her.

I pull back, her breath coming in desperate pants that puff warmth against my skin. I hold her perfectly still and just out of my reach.

"What's your plan, honeybee? How are you going to

make things right?" She has abso-fucking-lutely nothing to her name. Unless...

"I c-c-could d-dance." Her eyes dart away from mine and I give my fist a little shake, tugging on her hair to get her attention back where it belongs. On me. "At the Honey Pot, I mean. I, um, I think tips might be better there than at the diner?"

Would they fucking ever.

This beautiful young thing taking her clothes off and dancing on stage...she'd be flush with cash. And the regulars at the strip club her parents ran would be beside themselves to get a glimpse of her. The thought of that has my jaw clenching hard enough to crack a tooth. I don't like it. Not one bit. Those dirty old fuckers don't have any right to lay eyes on her, let alone touch her while tucking their filthy cash into her G-string.

No. Just, no.

"Absolutely not. With the time that's passed, the interest that has already accrued, you're going to need something more." Are my intentions pure? Not at all.

"More? I'll give you all my tips. All of them. Please, Christophe," she pleads, and goddamn, do I love the sound of her begging.

I fucking want more of that. I want to hear her beg from the floor, on her knees in front of me. But I can't let her strip. I can't handle that, sharing any part of this girl. What is she doing to me?

"Even if you supplement that income on your back, you'll never make enough to be free and clear. The only thing that might get you enough funds is if you were still a virgin and sold that prize to the highest bidder." The remark is flippant and completely off the cuff, but the way she steps back, red flush creeping up her delicate neck tells me I hit a mark. And I hit it *hard.*

Winnie wraps her arms around her middle. She hitches one foot up and places it on the far side of the other, crossing her legs. Protecting the only thing she has of value. And that is one valuable fucking commodity.

"How old are you?" I ask, swallowing the rest of the whiskey from my glass. I know...I do, but I want her confirmation.

"I'll be twenty-two next week," is all she says. And the way her voice breaks at that does things to me that I'm not sure I want to address.

"And what are you not telling me, honeybee?" I crowd her, obliterating the meager space she put between us. "Are you saying you're pure? Untouched? That your sweet virgin cunt has never been breached?"

Her eyes close as she takes a shaky breath. She's uncomfortable. She's doing everything she can to avoid me.

"I guarantee, *chère*, you can't escape me. There is no getting away from this. Answer the question—are you a virgin?"

Her nod is almost imperceptible. Almost, but I see it. I see every single move she makes. Every emotion that crosses her face. Everything.

"What have you been waiting for, honeybee? Anyone in particular?"

She bites her lower lip and tries her best to look away from me, to escape, but she is in my sights and there is no way for her to avoid me.

"Who have you been waiting for? Who were you keeping yourself pure for, sweet thing?" The flush of pink spreading up from beneath the modest neckline of her dress is mesmerizing. "Was it me? You been waiting all this time for me to bust your cherry?"

God fucking dammit...is this real? How is she a goddamn virgin? If that's the case, I don't know that I can hold myself in check. To be her first...her only. To show her all the things she's been missing. To teach her what pleasure is. Coach her on how to breathe through her nose—that she won't actually die as she gags on my dick. That her orgasm, *le petit morde,* can be reward enough for her efforts.

I want to guide her in her fucking sexual awakening.

Fuck my life, because I sure as shit know that I cannot let anyone else claim that prize.

"Tell me you've been saving yourself for me."

She takes a deep, bracing breath and sets her shoulders before responding. "No. Never. Anything I felt for you was stupid—a child's fantasy. It was nothing."

"Nothing? Never?" I say, my voice rumbling deep in my chest. "I call bullshit."

I'm desperate to feel the heat radiating off of her body. The electric buzz of her excitement mixed with her fear of the unknown. The fear and trepidation of losing the one thing that she has that's worth a fucking thing.

"Whatever I felt for you was the figment of a child's imagination. The absolute naivety of a first crush, nothing more. And it's gone, destroyed by the flames of humiliation of unrequited first love."

First love? The fuck is she talking about? No twelve-year-old kid has the tiniest inkling of what love means. Hell, at almost thirty, I don't know the first thing about it. Other than the fact that it's a bargaining tool. Leverage to be used by my enemies. It's nothing but a fucking weakness to be exploited by whoever wants to put me down. And there is no shortage of people with that high on their wish lists.

"That's how you feel, huh?" I ask. "No lingering

feelings here? Nothing?" I run the back of my knuckles from her cheek, down the delicate column of her throat and across the swell of her tits. "How pure are you, honeybee? Has anyone touched you here?"

She shifts, but there is nowhere for her to go, no space for her to retreat.

I trace the trail I want to lick down her flat belly and across her hips, skimming her pussy, through the thin fabric of her dress. "Has anyone tasted you?"

White, even teeth dent her plush lower lip as she tries to suppress a shudder.

"Did some pencil-dicked boy grope at you, fumbling his way across your luscious body? Whispering promises he could make you feel good but failing miserably? Is that why you're so pristine?"

I reach inside the slit of her wrap dress and graze the useless scrap of cotton. Her panties are soaking wet. The more I talk and taunt her, digging at her obvious lack of experience, the harder my dick gets. The more I want that first taste all to myself.

I push the crotch of her panties to the side and slide my fingers through her silky, wet heat, gathering the undeniable proof that she's aroused. That on at least the basest level, she wants me.

I move my free hand to cup her tit, dragging my thumb across her peaked nipple.

Eyes hooded.

Lips pursed.

"Christophe, please."

"Please what?"

"Stop."

I lift my gaze to meet hers, tears bright in her eyes threaten to spill over and tumble down her cheeks. The path my thumb traces back and forth has her mouth falling open and a breathy gasp spilling from those perfectly plump lips. "You don't like that? Your body's saying different," I taunt, stuck between the heat expanding through my body and the need to keep my heart cold, distant.

"If...if this is all I have that's worth anything, you can't..." She presses closer to me as she verbally pushes me away. "Don't take that from me. Please."

She's right. She's so fucking spot on, and I have to fight to dial myself back. Get my dick under control.

I cup and mold her breast in my palm, pinching her nipple one more time before releasing her and putting some distance between us. Winnie smooths her dress back in place as I turn and stalk back to the crystal decanter, splashing another healthy measure of whiskey into my glass. Casual. Aloof. Unaffected, like groping a veritable stranger is my God-given right. Hell, it's not unheard of in my world.

I slip my mask back into place and take a sip, rolling the amber spirit around on my tongue before swallowing.

Like it or not, I have to stay focused on getting what I need, not what I want. I fucking hate it when those two things don't line up or come neatly packaged together. Some shit about having my cake and eating it too. I never really understood that saying, but now...makes perfect sense. Because I want to devour Winnie, lick her, eat her, taste the sweet perfection of her.

The scent of her arousal is subtle on my hand. Sweet. Musky. I drop my middle finger into my glass and swirl the whiskey around until it coats my finger, mixing with her essence.

The heady combination of Winnie and whiskey is intoxicating. Addicting. It's distracting in the best possible way.

I coat my lips with her and smirk at the reflection in the window.

Winnie's fingers rest lightly against her lips like she's intrigued.

"Want a taste?" I ask.

Her head slowly swings left to right, but the look in her eyes is in direct opposition to that negative.

I suck my finger clean, making sure to lick the rest of her off my lips. *Fucking delicious.*

I expect her to blush more, to hide her eyes from me. To retreat and curl in on herself with embarrassment. So, when she closes the distance between us, I'm more than a little surprised.

She wraps her hand around the crystal glass and takes it from me, tipping it back and draining it. The bob of her delicate throat as she swallows just about has me coming undone. She presses the back of her hand to her mouth—holding the liquor in or trying to smother the burn, I don't know.

I smirk. "You going to make it?"

Her hand is a blur launching the glass to the hearth —shattering on impact as Winnie lifts her chin defiantly. Daring me to...what? What does she think I'm going to do? Slap her? Yell? Punish her?

I'm down with spanking her pert little ass until the skin is pink and hot, but that would just lead to me fucking her. Fantastic short-term, but not going to get me what I need. Instead, I clue her in on my plan.

"There's an auction."

Chapter 8

Desperation

Winnie

MY HEAD IS SPINNING. SPINNING.

This whole day, the entire week has been ridiculous. But *that* conversation—encounter?—with Christophe is next-level fucked up.

I need to get away. Put some space between us so I can think, because there is no way I'm going to let him auction off my virginity to make amends for my parents' stupidity.

They were addicts.

They were dealers.

They were idiots.

I knew growing up that they weren't normal, that they were terrible parents, but I had no idea they were...*this.*

That they'd gotten involved at this level.

That their consumption had taken over completely. But it had. And now it's bled over, staining my life with the detritus of their bad decisions. *As if they hadn't screwed me over badly enough...*

I pace back and forth across the suite of rooms I was shown to after Christophe blew my world apart with his mention of an auction—*the* auction. Because, evidently, this is a major event at the club my parents ran that I had no idea existed. Why would I? I've focused my entire life on avoiding the things that hide in the shadows. The dark, scary parts of the world that house true evil.

The plush carpeting silences my repetitive steps, allowing me to hear even the tiniest of noises out in the hall as I pace the length of the sitting room. I stop dead in my tracks as footsteps approach the door. My locked door, because let's not mistake this for anything other than what it is—I'm a prisoner here.

After a soft knock, the lock drags and clicks until the door pushes open revealing a kind faced gentleman in a perfectly fitted charcoal suit. The tray clutched in his arms is laden with covered dishes, a coffee carafe, and another glass of whiskey, but not in crystal. This one is in a plastic cup.

"Mr. Robicheaux said I'm not to trust you with the

good glassware. Though it does pain me to serve you a premium blend in what amounts to a child's sippy cup," the man says, his clear voice heavily accented, though it's very posh British as opposed to the lilt of French.

"Can you help me?" I plead. "I need to get out of here, find my friend. I think there's been some kind of misunderstanding. I don't belong here."

His wrinkled face pulls into a sympathetic smile. "Miss L'Ourson, I assure you that I cannot. Now, have a bit of a nosh, take a bath. Salts and essential oils are next to the tub, towels in the cupboard. And then relax. Crawl into bed and sleep. I'm sure you're exhausted." He sets his tray on the coffee table and fusses over the arrangement of its contents.

I can't do that. I don't know that my stomach could handle anything. Maybe the whiskey, but even that seems like a dicey prospect, not to mention I have nothing to change into. No clean clothes, and the last thing I'm going to do is hang out here, in Christophe's mansion, with nothing on. I need to be ready to escape if the opportunity presents itself. I don't know how I'll find Tru, but I will—I won't leave without her. I'll get us out of here and we'll run. For however long it takes, however far we have to go.

As if he's reading my mind, the gentleman states, "There's a robe, perhaps a few other things in the wardrobe, miss. Whatever plans you think you have, I suggest you forget them. It's a fruitless folly; you're here for the duration and I suggest you make the most of the amenities available while you're able."

I don't like what he's hinting at, but sage advice is sage advice.

"I'm at a complete disadvantage," I tell him as I edge toward the door. Maybe he left it unlocked, and I can slip out and run.

"How is that, Miss L'Ourson?"

As if there aren't a thousand different ways that I'm on the struggle bus here. "You know who I am, but I have no idea who you are."

One step toward the door.

Two.

Shifting my weight from one foot to the other grants me maybe another half step closer to freedom.

Tsk tsk. "No need to try and distract me, miss. You'll find that the reward is not worth the risk. Mr. Robicheaux has your room under guard, not to mention the cameras throughout the estate. Should you run, you'll be found immediately and returned to your suites." He pulls the cover from one of the dishes on his tray. "A proper meal for you or perhaps something lighter? A charcuterie?"

"I—" My protest is cut short.

"Garrick."

I shake my head, not at all sure I'm following. "What?"

He gives me a proper bow, one hand on his stomach, one on his back. "My name, miss. Bartholomew Garrick Hedgeworth. I am pleased to be in your service."

My head spins.

My knees wobble.

And I have to fight the urge to slump down to the floor and cry. I don't have time to cry. Where was this sting behind my eyes and burn in my nose when I needed it for the cops and the damn funeral?

I was close, so damn close to getting out of this town. To getting away from my parents and their pull on me. So close to finally being free.

The support of a warm hand on my elbow brings me back to the shitty reality that is now mine to deal with. If we were anywhere else, I would think Bartholomew Garrick Hedgeworth was a sweet older gentleman, maybe even Santa himself.

But we're here.

And I can't leave.

I allow him to guide me to a chair in front of the fireplace.

I accept the plate of food he hands me.

I wrap my fingers around the cup of whiskey, the

plastic bending and popping under the pressure of my grip.

How is it that I've jumped out of one fiery hell and straight into another? All my hard work, all the money I've saved, the plans I've made—for what? It's all been for nothing because I don't think there is any way out of this mess.

"Shall I draw you a hot bath, miss? A soak might do you well before you retire. Wash away the day and set all your wrongs to right." With a gentle prod, he nudges the cup to my mouth, *tsking* again and murmuring about blasphemy. "A sip and a bite of something, miss."

I'm not thirsty, certainly not hungry, but I can either fall apart in front of a complete stranger or I can cowgirl up and figure out what comes next. Since it's a fact that I do my best thinking while marinating in steamy water, I do what he asks. I pick at the plate, tasting nothing as I chew and swallow.

"A bath sounds good."

"Very good, miss."

With a perfectly executed bow, Garrick ducks into the ensuite. Several minutes later, he returns, announcing, "Your bath is ready. I've taken the liberty of adding salts to the water—lavender and honey, for the lady." I swear he holds his breath until I nod my agreement. Then he continues, "Towels are in the warmer, and I've hung a robe by your dressing table. If there's nothing else?"

The lady. Your dressing table.

At a loss for words, I shake my head and set the still-full plate on the coffee table.

He says, "Very well, then," as if everything is indeed very well.

Spoiler Alert: it's not.

Nothing is well. It's not good, not even okay. But the minute the door closes, and the lock clicks into place, I rise to my feet, grabbing the plastic cup of whiskey from the serving tray, and shuffle toward the bathroom.

Steam swirls above the copper soaking tub, the heavy scent of lavender filling the air.

I quickly disrobe, leaving my clothes in a pile on the floor. I would happily burn that black dress just to ensure that I never have to see it again, but it's the only thing I actually own here.

The water is perfect with the temperature straddling the line between too hot and just right. It takes a minute of easing each body part in, retreating, and trying again until I sink down and let the hot water suck the tension from my muscles. My skin turns pink where it's submerged, my cheeks, I'm sure, going rosy as they glisten with a sheen of sweat.

It feels glorious.

I close my eyes and breathe deeply allowing my head to rest on the raised lip of the basin. What am I going to do? How the hell am I going to get out of this?

I know my crush on Christophe was just that—puppy love. After he left and years later after I'd made peace with what I thought was a wildly broken heart, I figured I'd never see him again. That he was gone from my life and that was okay, right? I was a *child* and Christophe wasn't much younger than I am now.

But he's back.

And all grown up.

Sweet and caring no more, now Christophe is a freaking enigma.

Whether that's a good thing or not, I have no idea, but he sure is pretty to look at.

Pfft. A man like that isn't pretty.

Powerful.

Masculine.

Virile.

Fuck-hot is the most accurate term I can think of.

I envy his obviously custom-tailored shirt for how much contact it has with him. The solid mass of muscle when he pressed up against me, the way he moved me, commanding my body, was like nothing I've ever experienced.

Of course I've never experienced that. Because of

where I grew up, and how, I shut myself away. I kept my circle small. But that doesn't mean I'm not affected.

With the hard planes of his muscle-packed body front and center in my mind, I let my hand drift down beneath the steaming water to my center.

My fingers are a poor substitute for his blunt, thick digits. I dip and swirl, circling my clit, but all it manages to do is frustrate me.

Desperate for release, I mold and squeeze my breast, pinching my nipple hard between my thumb and fore-finger. Finally, my muscles tighten, my orgasm building as I pluck and pinch at my nipple, fingers flying against my clit. Bliss is so close—so damn close it's *right* there.

Right fucking there.

I moan, reaching...grasping at the release I need more than my next breath.

"Fuck."

The whispered curse is low enough, I can't be sure I actually heard it. But my eyes fly open, and I sit up so fast, water sloshes over the side of the tub, splashing on the black tile floor.

A hint of movement by the bathroom door has me crossing my arms over my chest.

Reflected in the shower glass is the unmistakable image of Christophe.

My captor.

The man who's been starring in my dirty mental porn reel.

"Don't let me interrupt you," Christophe drawls like there's not a thing out of the ordinary with him watching me in the bath.

It should bother me. I should be mortified at being caught with my hand in the cookie jar.

I should want to lash out at him for barging in here.

I should, but I don't.

*Spoiler alert...*I'm tired of being ruled by what I *should* do. It's not like it's done me any good up until now.

"Sweet and shy," he says to my silence—my perceived paralysis could totally be taken as embarrassment. His eyes are dark, scanning my exposed skin, lingering on where I'm doing a shit job of covering myself.

My nipples are pebbled, my skin tight. A flush spreading everywhere. I sink deeper into the water but there's nowhere for me to hide. I close my eyes and contemplate just going under and letting the water consume me, but I doubt Christophe would allow it.

His dark chuckle sends goosebumps skittering across my skin. "Want help or should I just let you finish on your own?"

I squeeze my eyes shut even tighter and dip my chin

below the water until I hear his footsteps retreating. When I chance a look, all I see is the blur of fine black trousers and a fitted white dress shirt before the doorway is empty again.

The scent of his cologne hangs heavy in the humid air swirling around me. Teasing me. Caressing me.

My thighs are slick with arousal and my body is thrumming with want. I'm closer to coming now, just from seeing Christophe—smelling him, having him in the room with me—than I was when my fingers were a blur on my body.

I slide my hand down, between my legs and with his gorgeous face in the forefront of my mind, I come undone.

God, there is something wrong with me.

Chapter 9

Debacle

Christophe

twenty-two years old

Frustrated and annoyed that it took as long as it did to get back there, I was impatient as fuck to finally arrive. I wanted to bypass the house and go straight out to find Winnie, whether that was at her house or in the woods, I didn't know. I didn't care. I just knew I had to see her.

Four years was way too long to go without seeing her in person, making sure she was still there and was okay. Or at least as okay as she could've been.

"Stop here and let me out," I told my driver. "I want to walk through the woods, stretch my legs before meeting with *Oncle*."

The man was assigned to me by my uncle after my parents died. Uncle Alain said it was to keep me safe, said it was a combined position of driver and bodyguard.

I thought it was overkill and a pain in the ass.

"I'm afraid I can't do that. My orders are to bring you straight to the estate."

I didn't doubt that for a minute, but I wasn't happy. I'd been gone for what felt like forever and the only tie I'd had to Winnie was my college roommate, Teague, who'd checked in on her when I couldn't. And I didn't like the things I'd heard recently.

The car stopped in the circle drive outside my uncle's estate, and I stepped out without waiting for the driver to get my door. I knew it bothered my uncle when I did shit like that, so in turn, it bothered the fucking driver because Uncle Alain believed strongly in shit rolling downhill.

I strode through the foyer waving off the butler and stalked into the study not waiting for an invitation. *Le Milieu*, and all of its holdings, was supposed to be mine.

Uncle Alain kept control way beyond what was necessary. At the time, I was thankful he'd stepped in so

I could go to college and have that bit of normalcy in the throes of chaos, but I was ready to take my place.

"*Oncle*, I—"

He immediately cut me off. "Christo, sit. I'll be with you shortly."

Dismissed.

That was the way he'd been treating me since he stepped into my father's shoes. Talking down to me, pushing me to the side when he should be teaching me, showing me the ropes. Setting me up to take the role my father had told me would be mine.

He turned away from me mumbling in the wild mix of French and English he liked to use in order to keep me in the dark. I hated it. Had I had longer with my parents, I'd have been able to decipher his words a whole lot easier, but they'd been ripped away from me way before I was ready, and college French somehow didn't cover the colloquialisms that were rife in *Le Milieu*.

I lowered my gaze, shutting out as many distractions as possible and concentrated on the rapid-fire exchange. Bits and pieces filtered through, and I silently translated, filing them away: Henri, debt, the girl. Apparently, that specific girl was special, but when it came to my uncle, they were either special or not worth the dirt on the bottom of his shoe.

"Now, Christophe," he barked, startling me out of

my thoughts. "I need you to go to the Honey Pot and collect the cash."

My brows jumped. "You want me to do that? You have people to handle the drops." It was an insult, a slap in the face to send me on his shitty errands like that. "I'm here to start the transition, *Oncle*, not to do grunt work."

His fist landed with a thud on the surface of his desk, and he sneered at me. "You're too good to do the little things, you don't deserve to learn the big." Again with the condescension.

It wasn't like I hadn't been running with the *beaux voyous* during my breaks from college. I was graduated now, ready for more. But it was day one. I'd do what he wanted first, prove once again, that I was capable, and then work my way in.

I shook my head and stood, buttoning my suit jacket as I stalked for the door. "I'll do the drop. Get the cash. But after, we talk."

He graced me with a very French shrug, one that was haughty and dismissive all at once.

Whatever. He wouldn't be able to avoid me any longer. I was there now, no other obligations, prepared to take my place in the organization. And maybe—hopefully—I'd find Winnie and see for myself that she was okay.

The town car stopped in the side alley next to the

club run by Henri and Claudette L'Ourson. The Honey Pot was on the seedy side, offering just about any vice a person could want. Booze, drugs, and women. Card games in the basement, and private rooms in the back that had seen more jizz than a sperm bank.

We owned much nicer clubs, cleaner with higher class, wealthier clientele. But for some reason, Uncle Alain was obsessed with that shit hole. The *why* had always baffled me.

When I stepped out of the car, the stench of piss and vomit hit me, curling my lip in disgust. One of the first things I'd do when I took full control would be to board that place up, burn it to the ground. I hated that Winnie's parents were the ones who'd been running it. That they were the ones who made it the sleazy mess that it was. Thank Jesus, they hadn't dragged her in.

The inside wasn't any better than the exterior and I made damn sure not to touch anything as I made my way to the office. Not a door, not a wall, nothing.

The office was empty, and while it would've been a major power move to make myself comfortable behind the desk, I didn't want to touch any of those surfaces either. I didn't want to think about the things that likely happened in that chair and on the desk, the DNA lodged in the crevices and soaked into the seams.

The rumble of pissed-off voices mixed with pounding feet preceded the thin, wiry ghost of a man that was Henri L'Ourson.

"What the fuck are you doing leaving strangers in my office without a man watching?" His voice was as high as he generally was, brimming with misplaced authority and false confidence.

Once he'd paused long enough for it to register just exactly who'd been left unattended in his office, his steps stuttered to a halt. His eyes shifted, darting around the dingy room as if he was looking for another body.

Uncle Alain had given no indication that there would be anyone else here; it was a simple cash exchange. If he'd thought anything odd might have been going down, he'd have sent me with some of his men.

"You're alone." It wasn't a question, but there was surprise behind the statement.

"I just need to collect the deposit, and then I'll be out of here." It took serious work not to tell him just how vile his establishment was.

Henri slunk behind the desk, his goon following close behind. Fool left me an easy way out. Not that I planned on needing an escape, but the lack of physical security displayed blew my mind. It was something I'd need to fix sooner as opposed to later.

A fine sheen of sweat glistened at Henri's temple as he pasted a tense smile on his face. "I... You're not who I expected. Give me a minute, let me go and uh, make sure we've got enou—" He caught himself, but it was obvious he was scraping the bottom of the barrels to make the payment.

Shaking his head, he glanced at the screen of his computer. His eyes went wide and he mumbled an apology before hoofing it out of the office.

Whatever he'd seen spooked him.

Curiosity got me and I rounded the desk. The security camera at the back of the club showed a man talking to my driver. Off to the side stood a girl in her mid-teens awkwardly shifting from one foot to the other. She was nervous, and she should've been. Nothing good happened in the alley behind the Honey Pot and she was way too fucking young to be standing there with those two men.

Henri shoved through the back door as the man handed a folded wad of cash toward the girl as he wrapped his meaty hand around her upper arm. It wasn't a protective gesture but a controlling one. Henri swiped the cash from the girl's hand and as she spun I got a good look at just how young she was, how pissed she was at him.

I watch as she argued with Henri, hands flying in the

air as if she was trying to make a point. What I saw when she turned to fully face the camera had my blood running cold.

Winnie L'Ourson was standing behind the shittiest strip club in town exchanging cash for God knew what. And her father, her fucking father, was facilitating the entire thing.

My molars ground as I watched the three men argue over what I could only hope was a huge misunderstanding and not the sale of a young girl. But I knew better. The only thing that kept me from storming through the club to rectify the situation was seeing Winnie stalk off and climb into the car at the end of the alley, her best friend, Tru, behind the wheel. Tru boldly flipped the men off as she peeled away, hopefully stealing Winnie away to safety.

My driver got back into the car as the man argued with Henri, obviously demanding his money back. He reared back to swing before Henri's man stepped in and caught the man's fist twisting it behind his back and shoving him against the trunk of the town car.

I counted the minutes until Henri reentered the office, shoving what looked a lot like that same wad of cash into a duffle before he handed it to me.

"What the fuck was that?" I asked still standing behind the desk.

Henri glanced from the monitor to a spot on the wall behind me. "Just a last minute transaction to pad the deposit. Nothing for you to concern yourself with."

"Oh, I'm concerned, Henri. You selling underage girls in broad daylight?" Time of day didn't bother me; the age of the girl was an issue. The specific girl he was trying to sell was a big fucking problem, but I wasn't ready to lay down my cards just then.

He scoffed as if none of that was reason to be concerned. "My daughter is my business. It's more than time to bring her into the family business, start earning her keep."

My vision went hazy with thoughts of murder. "What?"

He shrugged. He fucking shrugged as if she meant nothing to him. "She's been doing drops for me for a while, but she's worth some serious money now. It's about time to bring her in to work with Claudette's girls."

"Who was that out in the alley with her?" I needed a name so I could make sure he knew that she was untouchable.

"Paulo? One of the Italian's men. Likes 'em young but not inexperienced, you know? Likes the illusion that he's showing them the ropes without the bother of having to truly break them in." He turned and slunk away down the dark hallway, disappearing before I could put my fist through his face.

I searched the main room, down a handful of hallways and into rooms I'd never had any desire to visit, but Henri was nowhere to be found. Not that he was going to tell me anything good or honor any promise I might have been able to squeeze out of him. He wasn't an honorable man.

Instead, I returned to the car, tossing the duffle into the backseat and climbing in after. I grabbed my phone and hit Teague's number.

"I thought you said she was safe," I barked in lieu of a greeting.

"She is. I just checked in on her last week," he replied.

"Yeah? Well, I just saw her doing a deal for her old man and that fucker is getting ready to put her out there on the market."

"Christophe, I swear to God—"

"Hold on." I dropped the phone to the seat next to me and directed my driver, "Pull over."

I pushed out of the car and was on the guy from the alley in a matter of seconds. I'd assumed he'd gotten in a car and took off after Henri dismissed him, but there that fucker was walking down the street like he didn't have a care in the world.

Blood flew from his lip as he stumbled back from the impact of my fist. Before he had a chance to recover, I had him tucked away around the side of a building, my hand at his throat holding him in place.

"We have a fucking problem, Paulo." I said it conversationally, like we'd known each other for ages. Like we were equals, when we were decidedly not.

"What problem? We got no problems, man. I don't got a problem with you," he said, his words rasping across the palm of my hand.

I looked down at him and squeezed cutting off the rest of his bullshit. "The girl in the alley. That's where our problem lies, my friend, with the L'Ourson girl. She is absolutely off limits, understand?"

"The little bitch? She owes me—"

I squeezed again. "She owes you nothing. You have a problem with what went down back there, you take it up with her father. If I hear of you messing with her again, this problem between us is going to come to a head, and I promise, that's not something you want to be a part of, *comprenez-vous?*"

"I just want my money back. I deserve—"

Yep, I cut him off again, but that time with my fists until he slumped to the pavement. "This is what you deserve, nothing else. And if I find out that you or anyone touches that girl, I will hunt you down and kill you. You put the word out that she's not to be touched. You make sure the rest of the shit like you knows the score."

I pulled my pocket square free and wiped the blood from my knuckles.

Chapter 10

Darkness

Christophe

MOTHERFUCKER. WINNIE'S GOING TO BE THE DEATH
of me. The goddamn death of me.

My footsteps echo down the long corridor as I storm
out of her suite. I can handle a lot of things but having
her under my roof might not be one of them.

At the end of the hall, I turn left, back into the relative safety of my office. Not that this is where I want to
be. Fuck no. I would much rather be back in her bathroom, watching her pluck at her nipples and strum at her
clit, playing her body like an instrument to get off.

Who am I kidding?

I want to be the one playing with her. Winding her

up. Bending her over and sinking into her. Feeling her tight cunt strangle my dick.

I fill a fresh glass with whiskey and empty it twice, the memory of her scent lingering at the edge of my memory. *Fuck.* This is not how things were supposed to go. This was not my goddamn plan.

How, in the course of a moment, did I develop this gripping desire? This need for her? But, if I'm honest, it's been a hell of a lot longer than a moment. It's been there for a lifetime.

An eternity of watching over her, protecting her, making sure she had what she needed—at least that's what I thought I'd been doing. As it turns out, her parents were fucking that up too.

"Boss?"

I startle at Teague's tone.

"Sorry to... Did you jump?" he asks, brows high.

I glare at him and shake my head. "What?"

Teague laughs, low and full of disbelief. "I called your name four times. What's got you so tied up in knots?"

"What do you need?" Ignoring his question is the easier option by far.

"I mean, seriously. You look like you lost a game. Or like someone's playing keep away with your favorite toy." He's hit way too close to the truth with that observation.

I clench my jaw, the muscles jumping at the motion. "Do you have something to tell me, or are you just here to fucking comment on my countenance?"

The bastard smirks at me, like he knows something he's not supposed to. Like he can read me and knows where my mind is—who has a stranglehold on it.

With a sardonic laugh, he states, "I wanted to let you know the other girl is here."

"In a suite? Did she give you any trouble?"

He tilts his head and shrugs. "I had to call Hibou in to give her something to calm her down." Teague rubs a hand down his face, pulling at his short ginger beard. "She was a mess. Catatonic and then...I've never seen someone shake the way she did. It was—"

"But she's resting?" Winnie's friend may not be my main concern, but I can't have her in distress. No more than she would be in a situation like this, but that one is a wildcard. I'm glad he contacted the doctor I keep on retainer.

Teague meets my eye and nods once, his natural warmth flipping to icy protectiveness. He sinks into his stance, broadening his shoulders and flexing his hands. It's a flex, sure, but it's apparent he's staking his claim on her. One less thing for me to concern myself with.

"Good. Whatever she needs," I tell him. "And when she's up to it, take her to see Winnie, yes?"

"Of course." He lifts his chin and steps back toward the door. "You need me for anything?"

"No."

The single syllable barely tumbles from my mouth, and he's out of my office. Strong, steady steps echo behind him as he stalks down the hall—away from my office and toward the residential wing of the mansion.

I have no doubt that he's going straight to Tru's suite. I just hope he knows what he's getting himself into. I trust Teague with my life, but I need his head in my game, not bouncing around his own fantasies of playing hero with his little damsel in distress. Because there is not a single doubt in my mind that that girl is broken. Maybe beyond repair. Everything points to the fact that she's lost in a darkness I want no part of.

I step behind my desk and do a quick scan of security, checking camera feeds from around the perimeter of the property and systematically working my way into the interior feeds. I linger on the view from outside Winnie's suite.

The temptation to look inside is strong. There's one camera in the corner of her sitting room that offers a partial view into her bedroom. I should have planned better—held her up in my office longer so security could have added a camera to cover the full view of her room.

Fucking stupid.

Or maybe, just fucking psycho. From what I hear, the leap is not a long or particularly arduous one to make.

I pour a solid three fingers of whiskey into my glass and shut down my computer. I could drive myself off the deep end wondering—wanting—but I can't do that. I need to get my head in the game and lock down my next move.

Without a sound, I step out of my office and saunter toward my private rooms, though I deliberately pass the main staircase, winding through the hallways of the guest suites.

I pause outside her room and lift my glass to my lips. It has to be my imagination, no way it could still be lingering, but I inhale as I sip, pulling her scent deep into my lungs and savoring the memory of her taste.

Silence greets me as I stand, waiting, talking myself out of storming through the door and feeling her again firsthand.

Seconds turn into minutes before I finally step away and go find solace in my corner of the mansion.

The master suite takes up the entire wing above the guest suites. I shed my suit coat and loosen my tie, tossing the items to the sofa in front of my fireplace as I settle in. I pop the top buttons of my shirt and gaze out the floor-to-ceiling windows.

A full moon illuminates the dark night casting a cool glow on the woods lining the edge of the property. My gaze is drawn to where the tree—our gnarled oak—stands deep in the grove.

I walked away from her there, no intention of ever going back. Hell, it's been years, and I still haven't been back to that tree, but that doesn't mean I haven't kept it in my sights.

The longer I stare out into the dark and sip on my whiskey, the more I find my mind lingering on the woman sleeping below me. Did she finish what she'd started after I left her in the tub? Did she get herself off thinking of me or cursing me? Either way—as long as I was on her mind.

My dick thickens at the thought of her pinching her nipples, playing with her sweet pussy.

God, I want to dirty her up. Ruin her for everyone else. Fuck, the thought of another man touching her, tasting her, makes my blood run cold.

I pull my phone from my pocket and pull up the security feed on the app. The angle is shit; I can only see the top corner of her bed. But moonlight streams through the window, the beams casting half her face in shadow.

She rolls to her back, throwing an arm above her head, the other tucked beneath the covers, resting low on her stomach. The flimsy slip of a nightie she pulled on after her bath is twisted around her body, revealing the swell of her perfect tit. It would take no effort to snap the thin strap holding it in place. Barely a tug.

A normal person might think it's creepy that I'm standing here watching a pretty young thing sleep—that she's completely unaware of what's happening. But I'm anything *but* normal; I've proven that over and over and over again.

What normal person would walk away from an innocent child's crush only to resurface years later—after sending food when she needed it, money when it was scarce, keeping her safe—and tell her she's going to be sold at a skin auction? None. That person does not exist, because there's no way a rational, ordinary person would do that. Only a sick bastard could do those things, and on the day she buries her useless parents, too.

Yeah.

My eyes trace the moonbeams, lingering where they touch her skin. The curves and dips are nothing short of exquisite. Her nipples peak, the buds visible through the delicate fabric, almost as if a cool breeze is swirling through the room.

I want to wrap my lips around one and pull it into my mouth, sucking it deep. I want to trap the peak between my teeth and revel in the sounds my bite would pull from her. Something tells me it would become my favorite melody.

Blood rushes south, causing my dick to chub up. It's trapped at a bad angle, pressing painfully against the teeth of my zipper. And when I reach down to adjust it, I give myself a tight squeeze, not that it helps. The contact just makes me want her even more.

Since that can't happen, I free my cock from the constraints of fine Italian wool. I'm so hard I could drive a three-inch nail into a stud with both hands tied behind my back.

I spit in my palm and give myself a slow, firm stroke twisting around the head before sliding back down. I do it again, my eyes never leaving Winnie's image.

Giving in to the mental reel I have going of licking every inch of her body—nipping and biting at her tits, flattening my tongue against her pussy—is the only way I'll find any relief tonight.

I tighten my grip, squeezing my dick the way I imagine her tight heat would. Jesus, I've never fucked a virgin. Don't know that I could be patient enough not to just take her.

The thought of being anyone's first fuck is not some-thing that ever appealed to me. But being Winnie's? The first man to feel her from the inside...the *only* man to feel her wrapped around my cock... That is something I could get behind.

A groan slides up the back of my throat as my hand continues to abuse my dick. The base of my spine burns with the need to come. I drive the pace, faster and faster wishing it was Winnie's delicate hand—fuck, her mouth —stroking me.

I imagine sinking into her, pushing deep until my hips meet the backs of her thighs, my balls tight against her ass.

My head falls back, eyes half closed, as my hands tighten. I barrel toward a release that's not at all close to what I want. I growl my frustration as I blow my load, thick ropes of jizz painting the panes of glass in front of me.

I loosen my hold on my dick and tuck it away. My gaze drops to the floor. Winnie is maybe twelve—fifteen? —feet away from me and the only relief I got was from my own fucking hand. Disappointment isn't a strong enough word for what I feel.

I tilt my phone, still tightly gripped in my other hand. I want one more look at Winnie. Maybe having her image burned into my brain will allow me to find a handful of hours of sleep. If anything can bring me peace, it's her.

What I find on the security feed takes my breath away.

Instead of Winnie's sleeping form, relaxed and peaceful, she's staring at me through the screen. Her eyes wide, lips parted, almost as if she knows I'm watching her, that I just came harder than I think I ever have before.

And the smirk she's wearing, like she knows she nearly brought me to my knees.

Winnie

My locked door opens for the second time today, revealing the man who stole Tru away from me at the cemetery. He nods to me, staid and solemn, then steps to the side allowing me to see Tru, tear-stained and cowering behind him.

It's been almost twenty-four hours and she looks petrified, absolutely panicked.

"Tru," I say softly, not wanting to startle her. I can only imagine just how on edge she is right now. Call me a mother hen when it comes to her, but she hasn't spent a night away from my house since I got her back.

The years she was away—first stolen, then recovering—were absolutely hell for me. After Christophe disappeared, and my father started using me for his business deals, Tru was the only friend I had. Until she was gone too. What happened to her during that time...I don't know that I can ever fully understand it.

I get no reaction and step closer repeating her name and getting the same response. Non-response, really, because she gives me absolutely nothing.

I glare at her tall, copper-haired escort and whatever hate and vitriol is running through me, tempers just the tiniest bit. His stoicism is softened with the way he looks at her.

He offers me a small smile and ushers Tru through the door, settling her on the oversized chair angled toward the warmth and flames radiating from the fireplace.

"What did you do to her?" I bite out on a whispered hiss. "Where has she been?"

My instinct, my gut reaction, is to put myself between this guy and Tru. To protect her, shield her from everything and anything bad in the world. I failed her once, the thought of doing that again is unfathomable.

But I stop and look. Really take in the dynamic between them.

He's different—gentle, caring...attentive and in tune with the darkness that lives inside her, with her needs.

He shakes out the soft, thick throw from the back of the chair and tucks it around her, brushing her baby fine hairs back from her face.

There's something there—something more. Something *intriguing*, but I don't know that I have time to think about it now.

Later. Later, I'll try to parse things out, ask Tru...you know, when she's able to string together coherent thoughts and speak.

For right now, I'll let it go, at least this part of things. I need whatever information I can get from this guy, make a plan, and steal us away to safety.

"She's in shock, been shut down since I put her in the car."

I don't miss the tender way he strokes her hair, runs his knuckles down her cheek, the side of her neck. The softening of his eyes as his gaze roams, touching her everywhere.

"Why are you just now getting here? Where did you take her?" I push my way to Tru's side and drop to my knees in front of her.

She's here, but she's not present. For years, I've done everything I could to protect Tru from the outside world. Soothe her anxieties, keep the scary monsters and things that go bump in the night far, far away from her.

"She—"

I cut him off. "And who are you? What's your name?"

A muscle in his jaw jumps and his eyes narrow ever so slightly before he blows out a sharp breath. "Teague Grey. I work for Mr. Robicheaux," he states sharply. When his gaze darts back to Tru, it softens considerably. "Truie was...she was struggling when we left the cemetery. I drove until she calmed and then brought her here. I took her straight to her suite of rooms last night. I assure you; I saw to her needs personally."

My glare is so sharp, it almost shocks me not to see blood dripping from his eyes.

"You saw to her needs? If you hurt her...laid a single finger on her..." I can't even finish my thought.

This whole situation is so fucked up.

"Chr—Excuse me. Mr. Robicheaux asked me to bring her to see you as soon as possible today. She's... she's not yet eaten and needs to drink some water." Teague glances from Tru to me and asks, "If you could perhaps encourage her along those lines, I would greatly appreciate it. I have some things to see to for Mr. Robicheaux." He waits for my response before nodding once again and stepping out into the hall.

Garrick takes the ginger oaf's place, a heavy tray of food and drinks balanced expertly on his fingertips. "I've taken the liberty of bringing a simple tea. A bit early in the day, but it seemed prudent."

He presents a gorgeous spread of finger sandwiches, hand pies, and tarts. Cookies and delicate little cakes.

I've never in my life seen anything so lavish. He can't really think this is simple, can he?

Fine porcelain plates are set before us as well as crystal water goblets, but the cutlery is very obviously absent. Not that it's necessary for the food, everything is bitesize.

"Is it a special occasion?" I ask, my voice sharper than the sweet man deserves.

"Miss?" He pauses in his ministrations, his brows pulled together. "It's truly a simple offering. Mr. Robicheaux didn't want your dinner spoiled. Is it not to your liking?"

Lord help me, I feel like I'm in an alternate reality. Like the shit I saw my parents tripping through when they took too much of their own stash.

"Would the lady rather have something different? I'm happy to provide whatever it is you'd prefer." He stands ramrod straight and smooths his perfectly tailored jacket. The man is quite serious and now I feel like a bumbling idiot. A rude bumbling idiot.

"No, I'm sorry. Everything looks great, really. I just meant"—I point toward where my plastic cup from last night sits on the end table—"I'm being trusted with real glassware?"

A grin pulls at the corner of his mouth. "It would seem so, miss. Is there anything more I can do for you? For Miss Cochonette?"

"You're still opposed to leaving the door unlocked and letting us sneak out of here?" I know the answer is no, but it can't hurt to try.

"I see the lady has a lovely sense of humor today." He steps to the door and before locking us in tight, adds, "Dinner is at eight. Mr. Robicheaux will expect you to dress for the occasion."

Hours later, after spending most of the afternoon with Tru, watching movies and doing everything in my power to coax some water into her, she's asleep. Curled into a tight ball tucked into my massive bed, the throw Teague placed over her gripped securely in her balled fists.

Each time I moved the throw, Tru pulled it back in tighter, but of the handful of words she gave me, not a single one gave me anything about where she spent last night. Not a word about what happened or why she's been shaking so hard.

All I've gotten from her at the mention of Teague is

the smallest pause in her trembling as she clutches the last thing he touched to her chest.

I glance at the clock and curse the fact that I can't just stay here with her. I'm exhausted and the last thing I want to do is squeeze myself into the scrap of a dress that was delivered to my room.

It's gorgeous—bloodred and cut to mold to my curves.

Grudgingly, I shower and dry my hair, twisting it into space buns perched on the crown of my head. As I dust on makeup, I wonder who went shopping for all of this and exactly how they matched my colors so perfectly.

And why.

Why is any of this happening? There has got to be more than meets the eye.

I don't doubt that my parents fucked up and did it spectacularly. They've been doing that my whole life. But this attention from Christophe, his intensity, is unlike anything I could imagine. It's got to spring from something different, something deeply rooted and terrifying.

Jesus.

I pause, makeup brush smooshed against my cheek. What the hell am I doing? After all that I've been through and as crazy as all of this has been, why am I painting my face fully intent on stepping into a dress that was delivered to my room? My locked room in this damn house?

Stockholm Syndrome is a very real thing, but that doesn't mean I have to drink willingly from its cup.

Hell no.

I set the high-end products aside, adjust the belt on my robe and glare at the gorgeous gown hanging from the door of the closet. While it hasn't done anything to me, what it represents has me all kinds of twisted up.

I've never really rocked the boat, always did what was expected of me. Toed the line to keep things copacetic and not make waves no matter what sketchy situation my father happily sent me into. Fat lot of good that did me.

Instead of sliding the shimmery red gown on, I dig through the other clothes tucked neatly away in the walk-in closet. If I'm going to be waltzing into the unknown with this dinner, I want my armor to be comfortable.

Tiny black workout shorts that will barely cover my ass. I dig through another drawer and find a fitted t-shirt almost the exact color of the dress. I pull each item on, adding a pair of soft socks that hit just above my knees.

I don't even bother with the full-length mirror

leaning against the wall. I feel cute and comfortable—and totally inappropriate for a formal dinner.

I love it.

There's a soft knock before the lock clicks and the door swings open. Garrick steps into the suite and clears his throat, glancing around fleetingly. I can only imagine his trepidation.

I enter the sitting room and pull the bedroom door closed behind me. Tru is well and truly out cold and if she stays that way, it'll make my life so much easier. I'll be able to concentrate on finding a way out of all of this.

"Miss L'Ourson? Was there a problem with your attire for the evening?" Panic laces the butler's question, concern marring his features.

His eyes sweep me up and down, taking in my hair, my outfit, my knee socks. I look more like I should be starring in a sorority porno than having dinner in a mansion with a beautifully dangerous specimen of a man.

"Nope, no problems. I decided this is more...me." I pluck at the hem of my t-shirt, tugging the cropped fabric low enough to reveal the swell of my tits. There's not much to it, honestly. My choices are flashing under-boob or ample cleavage.

Garrick's eyes widen the slightest bit before his gaze

darts to whatever is over my shoulder. That blank wall must be fascinating with the way he's focused.

"I see"—he clears his throat and straightens his spine—"Mr. Robicheaux specifically requested you dress."

"He did. You mentioned that earlier. But here's the thing, Garrick. I don't see why I should put in the effort. Why should I go through all the work of doing my hair and makeup? Why should I stuff myself into a dress that may not even fit me—"

"I assure you, miss, the dress is to your exact measurements."

"When I am nothing more than a hostage here?" I ignore the fact that someone involved not only picked up the perfect makeup palette but also knows my measurements. That's just a whole different level of...I'm not sure what.

"Miss, I implore you." Garrick is the epitome of stoicism as he dutifully avoids actually looking at me. Once again, the blank wall over my shoulder is getting the full weight of his stare. "Mr. Robicheaux is—"

"Going to have to get over himself," I tell him with a smirk. "Now, are you escorting me to face my sentence? Or are you going to bring me another charcuterie board and some wine? Because that sounds so much better than whatever Christophe has in store for me. I think I'd much rather hang out with you and Tru, shooting the shit and painting each other's nails."

"As delightful an evening as that may be, your presence has been requested in the dining room. And I rather enjoy the state of my being just as it is," he states, fighting the lift at the corner of his mouth.

Garrick opens the door and ushers me out into the hallway.

Teague looks up from his phone, eyes bright, shoulders shaking in silent laughter.

He looks almost pained, holding back his smile as he takes me in. "Shit. I hate that I'm going to miss the boss's reaction to this."

I laugh. "You're not joining us for dinner?"

He shakes his head, letting a small chuckle escape. "Nah. Much as I'd love to see Christophe's face when you waltz your ass into the dining room, I don't want Tru to wake up alone." He pushes into my suite and opens the door separating the bedroom from the sitting room. His features soften as he gazes at Tru's sleeping form. The door stays ajar as he pads silently to the settee, settling in as if there's no other place he'd rather be.

And I hate him a tiny bit less for the way he cares for my friend.

Chapter 12

Downfall

Christophe

She's trying to kill me.

She's trying to fucking kill me.

Garrick cringes at the daggers shooting from my eyes, but Winnie just tips her lips into a ghost of a smile. Like she knows what she's doing to my goddamn blood pressure.

Instead of the dress I arranged for her this evening, she has the nerve to show up in booty shorts and a fucking cropped top. Not only is the swell of her ass cheeks in full view, but the curve of her tits is also there for all the world to see. And of course. Of-fucking-course, she's not wearing a goddamn bra. Or panties that I can see, for that matter.

She might as well have walked into the room wearing nothing at all.

I grind my teeth, my molars nearly cracking from the pressure. One step toward her, turns into two, then three before I'm brought up short.

"Not like you to bring entertainment to the house, Christo," my uncle, Alain, rumbles as he pulls the thick, foul-smelling cigar from his teeth. "But I like what I see."

I watch, unmoving as his eyes rake over every inch of her, lingering on her barely covered ass before going straight to her tits.

The man is disgusting.

He takes what he can and uses it until there is nothing left. Drugs. Businesses. People. *Women*. It doesn't matter what the commodity or who he makes suffer. In fact, I think the suffering is his favorite part.

He made my father suffer every day before he was gunned down. I watched Alain twist the figurative knife in my father's back, threaten, complain. Caused shit to sour at every opportunity.

Now he's the head of our family.

I was too young to take over when my father died, so Uncle Alain stepped in to help. To teach me, guide me. He's gotten comfortable with being at the top, sloppy on occasion, but mostly just really comfortable.

But he's still a dangerous motherfucker.

I lock my shit down, smoothing all emotion from my face making it nothing more than a blank plastic mask. Winnie doesn't need to be on Alain's radar any more than she already is showing up here dressed like this.

Hell, if I had known he was coming to the house, I'd have kept her hidden away in her suite for the night. Maybe had Teague take her and her friend for a drive—to the next county over or maybe even another state. Anything to keep Alain at bay.

I can't spare the time to pick apart the reasons behind wanting to keep her far away from him. Not now. Not when it's going to take my full attention to distract my uncle. Because Winnie could very easily become my downfall.

I shift my weight and allow a lecherous grin to pull at my mouth. I have a role to play and a shit situation to finesse. "Had I known you'd be here tonight, *Oncle*, I'd have arranged for more entertainment. As it is, I planned only for myself."

The confidence Winnie wore strutting into this room wavers at the lurid insinuation in my words.

I narrow my eyes as she meets my gaze. I need her to feel the threat of the viper standing next to me and act accordingly. Just a hint of submission, that's all I need to get her out of this.

I drag my tongue across my bottom lip, tilt my chin

toward the door at the back of the dining room. "Why don't you wait for me in my office, doll? We can finish your interview when I'm done here," I tell her, my hand dropping to my belt buckle.

My dick is not going to get hard with my uncle in the same room, let alone within arm's reach. The motion is strictly to allude that her interview will be conducted on her knees.

Alain's paunch bounces as he chuckles darkly. "Let the *fille* stay while we eat. If she's good, we can both *interview* her. I don't mind sharing." He doesn't bother with a subtle adjustment. No, the bastard reaches down and strokes his puny dick through his suit trousers not giving a shit who gets to witness it.

Winnie's eyes widen as fear—disgust, more likely— flickers across her face. Her gaze lands on mine and I could be dreaming, it could be wishful thinking, but with just a look, she seems to get her shit collected and pulls her confidence back over her.

She's putting her trust in me.

It's foolish and misguided, considering I told her just yesterday that she's going to stand on the auction block for sick shits like my uncle to bid on, but here we are.

"No." I don't manage to keep all of the venom from that single word. And though I'm the one lacing my response with poison, I don't doubt for an instant Alain's bite will be anything less than fatal.

He makes that decidedly French noise, the one that conveys disgust, disappointment, or derision depending on what the situation calls for. He pulls his chair from under the table and shoots a glare my way.

"You have a lot of your father in you," he says, settling into the chair.

It should be a compliment.

From anyone else, that statement would be, but his tone is woven through with sharp, sinister threads.

Cold slides down my spine in warning, ice spreading through my veins.

He wraps his meaty hand around the delicate wine glass, the one that was supposed to be pressed against Winnie's plump, painted lips, not his. But there's not one fucking thing going according to plan tonight. "What are we eating, Christo? I'm famished." His implication is clear as his gaze drops to the apex of Winnie's thighs.

I drop into the seat at the head of the table, a position I'm sure it killed Alain not to claim, and spread my legs. Without even a glance in her direction, I pat my thigh and hold my hand out to Winnie.

For the beat of a heart, she hesitates, but then with a shaky swing of her hips, she closes the distance between us and perches her lush ass on my knee.

"Have dinner brought in, Garrick." My order is lazy and dismissive, as though I don't have a care in the world. But my hand is firm and possessive as I reach for Winnie's hip and pull her closer to me.

Alain watches the claim intently, a satisfied smile slashed across his face, interrupted only when he stuffs that fucking cigar between his yellow-stained teeth. He chuckles again and repeats his previous comment. "A lot of your father in you, boy."

We eat the dinner I had prepared for Winnie and me, my uncle ignoring the fact that I have a woman sitting on my lap through the meal.

I feed her in between my own bites. I'd insisted she come to dinner hungry. I won't make her stay that way.

Alain talks of nothing important, nothing that can't be overheard by someone outside the family. But his mind is working the entire time. I can practically see the gears turning as he ponders and sorts through the evening.

It's not until dessert that he takes visible notice of Winnie again. As I slide a spoonful of honey-sweetened galette past her luscious lips, Alain drops his spoon, sending it clattering against the plate.

His head pops up, gaze darting from Winnie to me and back again as recognition settles in. Whatever he's been ruminating over through the meal, it's finally clicked together for him.

He nods silently and pushes away from the table. Standing, he walks to the door without a word.

The silence is far more ominous than any threat he can issue. Though I know—*I know*—I haven't said Winnie's name, haven't alluded to who she is, Alain figured it out. Fuck me.

Winnie goes rigid and my fingers press hard into her hip, warning her not to react. She might be innocent in the most enticing way, but she's seen evil in the world. Hell, a rock could feel the danger hanging heavy in the air around us.

"Debts need to be collected; they cannot be allowed to stand. Took a long time for your father to learn that lesson. Don't make the same mistakes he did, Christo. It won't end any better for you." Alain stalks out of my dining room, tossing a final comment over his shoulder. "I'll see you both at the auction. Good evening, Miss L'Ourson."

Time ticks by in reverse, expanding to fill the void left by Alain's departure, as dread fights with fury. I hold my breath, my grip tightening even further on Winnie's hip as I wait to hear the click of my front door. Voices drift back, Uncle Alain and Teague, though neither speak loud enough for me to follow their conversation.

When the door finally clicks and footsteps drift away, I push to my feet, bringing Winnie with me.

"What the fuck were you thinking walking in here in that?" I grind out, tension electrifying me.

"Who was that? Why does he know who I am?"

Ignoring her rapid fire questions, I demand, "I sent a dress to your suite. Where the fuck is it?"

"You never said it. How does he know my name?" Her voice is sure though she's shaking so hard, her tits are quivering.

"Do you have any idea what you just fucking did?"

"What does he want with me?"

Each question is answered with another, rising in volume until our voices echo off the high ceilings. And with every non-answer I stalk away from the damn table, backing Winnie up until her trembling body is pressed between mine and the window.

She has to tilt her head back in order to see my face and, with her eyes wide and lips parted, she's a fucking wet dream.

I don't know if I want to throttle her for being so goddamn careless or strip her naked and fuck her up against the glass.

"Alain is my uncle and he's a bastard on his best day. I work for him." It kills me to say that aloud. I should be the one running this family, taking care of business.

"And he knows everything there is to know about people who owe him money. Your parents—"

Her gasp pushes her tits hard against my chest, cutting me off mid-sentence and scrambling my brain. Jesus, the feel of her body pressed against mine is enough to drive me insane, to make me think I'm fucking invincible.

My fingers dig into the ample swell of her ass as I palm it, pulling her closer still. I slide my free hand over the dip of her waist, higher and higher.

Her tiny, cropped shirt allows me easy access to her bare tit, the tight nipple beading up into a delicious little point.

I brush my thumb across the taut nub and fight the urge to bend and take it into my mouth. I want to lick it. Bite it. Suck on it until she comes from that alone.

There's no ignoring the effect she has on me. My dick is hard as steel, trapped between us and begging to come out and play.

She plants her hands on my chest and pushes against me in a feeble attempt to put space between us, not that it does her any good.

"You feel that, honeybee?" I grind my dick against her. "That's what Alain wants from you. He wants to fuck you. And when he finds out you're a virgin? He's going to do everything in his power to get you. He's going to make sure your pretty pussy is his for the taking, and then when he's done, when he is good and tired of you, he'll let his men have their turns." I wait for that chunk of information to sink in before I drive home the severity of Alain's depravity. "Who knows what'll be left of you when they're done." I stopped her from being used that way six years ago; there's no guarantee that I feel like being a hero again.

"What choice do I have?" she asks.

The strength in her voice surprises me. I would have expected her to crumble—fall apart at the picture I just painted.

She inhales deeply and then pushes the air from her lungs, her shoulders settling in resignation. "It's not the first time I've had to pick up the pieces of my parents' bad decisions. I know how this goes."

Jesus. Just when I thought she couldn't get any more alluring...

She has no fucking idea how this is going to go.

Chapter 13

Dire

Winnie

THERE'S NO CONVERSATION, JUST COLD, uncomfortable silence as Garrick escorts me back to my suite. Even the lock clicking into place seems quieter than usual, as if that inanimate object has somehow learned consciousness, become sentient. Like it's aware of just how dire my situation is.

How did I get here? How the hell did my life get to the place where I'm locked away in the mafia mansion of my childhood friend, staring down the barrel of a human auction that will hopefully net enough funds to clear my parents' ridiculous drug debt?

If I read this in a book, I would toss that paperback across the room and roll my eyes so hard, I'd strain something and end up with double vision. And one Christophe Robicheaux is more than enough, thank you very much.

"Is there anything I can get for you before you retire for the evening?" Garrick stands just inside the door, hands clasped behind his back.

If I thought for a moment that he was nothing more than a *normal* butler, I'd consider lunging at him, shoving him to the side and running for my life. But I seriously doubt he's simply a house servant without a special skill set that doesn't show up on a typical resume. And it's not just my life hanging in the balance, either.

My shoulders slump forward in defeat. I'll allow myself that, just for tonight, because I need a plan.

"Thanks. I'm just going to wash my face and pass out after I check on Tru." I take a step toward the bedroom and pull up short when Garrick makes a humming noise. "What?" I ask.

He shakes his head. "Miss Cochonette has retired for the evening."

My brows pull together as I cross the room, pulling up short at the sight of my empty bed. "Where is she?" I whip around to face him. Any tension I allowed to leach out only moments ago, is back. My hands fist and shoulders rise as every muscle in my body tightens and prepares to fight. "Who took her away from me?"

Tru needs me.

If I'm being honest, I need her, too. I'm comfortable taking care of her, looking out for her. Giving her a stable environment in which to heal as much as she can. It gives me a purpose beyond just me, something to work for. Planning for my exodus from this town was so much easier once I had another person to consider.

Without even realizing I'd moved, I'm across the room, looking past Garrick's rigid form into the hallway.

He places his hands on my upper arms and holds me in place. "She's in her suite of rooms, quite comfortable, I assure you."

I push against his hold, desperate to get to her. "You... No. You don't know what she's been through, Garrick. You don't know what she needs." What if she has an episode and goes catatonic again? She had finally settled and stopped shaking just before I left for the fucked up dinner with Christophe and his uncle.

I fully expected to come back and crawl into bed with her. That close, I might have gotten some sleep in bits and starts, but with her somewhere else in this gilded prison, somewhere that I can't hear her if she cries out, that I can't get to her if she needs me, any hope for me to drift off is gone.

This entire thing is a mess, and now I don't even

know where my friend is. Tears sting as they gather in my eyes.

"Would it soothe you to lay eyes on her before you retire, miss?" He gives my arms a subtle squeeze and dips slightly to put himself in my line of sight, gaining my focus. "I can escort you to her suite to set your mind at ease."

I blink back the tears that threaten to spill and ask, "Is that allowed?" When did things change so drastically that I'm asking permission to do anything? This is some serious bullshit.

Garrick smiles, his eyes crinkling with the shift of his cheeks. "It's not explicitly forbidden, but perhaps we'll keep this little fieldtrip between us, shall we?"

I pull in a shaky breath and let it out slowly while nodding. I'll agree to just about anything right now if it gets me to Tru.

"Right, then. If you'll follow me?" He releases his hold on me and steps back, sweeping a hand toward the hallway.

I follow him through an impossible labyrinth and push past him when he finally opens a door. The layout of the suite is similar to mine with a sitting room and a door that likely leads to the bedroom and ensuite beyond.

What I do not expect is the relaxed tiger of a man,

lounging on the settee that looks far too delicate to support his bulk.

Teague pushes to his feet, hand immediately reaching for the holster at his side. He darts his gaze over us, looking into the hall beyond when he detects no immediate threat from Garrick or myself. "What's happened?" he barks.

"Miss L'Ourson would like to see Miss Cochonette and ensure her comfort before retiring for the evening," Garrick explains.

I duck around the men and dart for the bedroom, closing and locking the door behind me. I'm sure they both have keys and would have no qualms about breaking through, if need be, but the symbolic security eases my nerves.

The lamp on the dresser casts a soft glow throughout the space giving me just enough light to see the silhouette of Tru's small form tucked beneath the mound of blankets.

I tiptoe across the room and slide onto the plush bed. Any worry of disturbing her with my movement dissipates; the mattress is so luxurious that there's no transfer of movement. Wispy, platinum blond hair rests on her cheek, rising lightly with each soft exhale.

Her features are as relaxed as I think I've ever seen them as she sleeps, the throw from my room still clutched in her fists, tucked up next to her face. She's okay. She's resting. I don't know how, after the upheaval from what has become our normal routine in the years that she's lived with my family. That routine was necessary when she was released to us. Change—the unknown—is not her friend.

I reach out and gently slide the hair off her face, tucking it away so I can really see her. So she's not hidden from me.

There are no salty trails from her early tears. She's fresh-faced and absolutely still, no trembling, no pinched lips, no tic in the muscles of her jaw.

I almost don't recognize her like this. It's been years since I've seen this side of Tru.

I've missed her. Missed the way she used to be...before.

The door cracks open, shitting all over my illusion of separation. Teague fills the space and after a moment, he silently demands that I leave Tru to sleep.

It goes against everything in me to leave her, but this is not the time to put up a fuss. Maybe I can confuse these men, throw them off their game by yielding when resisting won't get me anything in return.

I silently pad out of the room, noting that Teague's gaze stays on Tru well after I've brushed past him. Only when he's satisfied that my presence didn't disturb her, does he pull the door closed and turn to glare at me.

"Satisfied?" His voice is low and gruff, softened only by the slightest lilt of an accent.

My brows pop high. "I am. Why'd you move her though? She was fine with me in my room."

"I feel better having her here, with me." He folds his arms across his chest, settling into his heels.

I have no doubt that it would take a truckload of determination and a damn miracle to get through him to hurt her. But why?

"Where is this over-the-top protective shit coming from? What do you... If you touch her, if you lay one fucking finger on her, I'll kill you myself." How I'd accomplish that is a problem for future Winnie, but I don't tell him that because the way his head snaps back as if I've slapped him gives me pause.

He looks offended at my insinuation that he might harm her in any way.

"Settle down. The last thing I'd ever do is hurt Truie." He nods to Garrick, who steps out of the room, an amused smile pulling at his lips as he patiently waits for me to join him.

Whatever his reasons for attaching himself to her and sitting sentry outside her door, are something to think about as I lay in bed later, because I've officially been excused.

With my mind settled and my heart at ease knowing that Tru's okay, I pay careful attention on the return to my suite. The mansion is massive, but the winding labyrinth of our earlier trip is actually a couple of turns and three doors from the last of those.

I feel pretty confident that I can find my way back... if the opportunity presents itself.

"What's the plan for tomorrow?" I ask as Garrick ushers me into my sitting room.

His chuckle is soft, amused. "That, my dear, is up to Mr. Robicheaux. I don't deign to guess at his designs for the future." He moves through the rooms comfortably, clicking off lamps, pulling curtains closed, and ultimately turning down the covers on my bed. "If there's nothing further?" he asks, pausing by the chair that's been resituated in its original position.

"Thank you," I say, and I find that I sincerely mean it. As bad as the past day has been here, if it wasn't for Garrick's gentle nature, it would have been so much worse.

"Not at all, miss. Rest well," he says as if knowing that sleep isn't a given for me. "Until tomorrow."

I slump into the chair, my gaze settling on the glimmering silk of the window treatments. There's a gap where the curtains weren't pulled quite closed, and in the dark of the room, the moon casts a soft glow over the grounds.

The illusion of freedom pulls me from where I sit, and I find myself pushing through the curtains until I'm cocooned between the crisp silk and cool glass. I don't doubt that there are guards out there, at the very least cameras securing the grounds, but at the edge of the manicured lawn is a darkness that can only be attributed to thickly grown trees.

The woods.

Our woods.

And just like that, I find a glimmer of hope. I have no desire to run to the home I grew up in; it's never been a safe place. But it is familiar.

If I can find a way to get us out of here, I can get us home. And if I can get us home, freedom doesn't seem quite so unattainable.

Decadence

Christophe

Winnie stands wrapped in a cloak of silk curtains, lit by the moon as it streams through her window.

I don't know what she's staring at, if any of what's out there looks at all familiar to her since she's never been to my house. Would never come with me any of the times I asked her to follow me home from the woods. But the picture she makes stops my lungs, holding my breath hostage.

Her neck lengthens as she tilts her head to the side and unwinds the tight little twin buns. Waves glide down past the bottom of that tiny shirt, swinging against her back as she scrubs her fingers through the locks.

She arches, stretching her arms above her head, relieving tension that's obviously settled deep in her bones. Hell, the fact that she hasn't fallen apart is a testament to her strength.

I swirl my glass, ice clinking against the sides.

Last night, I sipped whiskey sweetened with her honey. The whiskey in my glass tonight falls sadly short.

I have work to do, emails to respond to, shit to take care of but none of that interests me. All I want is to sit here and stare at the picture of innocence bathed in silk and moonbeams.

That's a lie. I want to do a lot more than stare at her.

Before Alain barged in uninvited, I was fine—no, I was okay with doing what needed to be done. Debts are not allowed to stand, and selling her at auction is really the only way to clear what's owed.

After seeing the way he leered at her, hearing the way he wanted to use her, I was rethinking that plan.

The moment it clicked for him just exactly who it was perched on my thigh, my stomach dropped out my ass.

I didn't want to know what he was thinking, the vile thoughts running through his mind, but there was no doubt in my mind what they consisted of.

The things he would do to her, she'd never survive. And begging for death would get her nowhere. I told her as much, but seeing the glint in his eye, yeah, that was too much.

"You good, boss?" Teague stalks into my office and lowers himself into the chair opposite my desk.

When I don't answer, he tears his gaze from the screen of his phone and glances up at me. On my screen, Winnie pulls the curtains closed and leaves her sitting room. I want to follow her into her room, watch her strip off the day and slide between her sheets, but I don't need Teague's eyes on her like that. I'm the only one with access to the camera in her room. I plan on keeping it that way.

I had Teague pull her friend from her bed and take her back to her own suites so my men could work. I didn't like not being able to see Winnie last night. I stole down to her room in the middle of the night, just for another glimpse of her.

"Boss?"

I push the air from my lungs and glance out the window. "What did Alain say to you when he left tonight?"

A laugh huffs from him, though I'm fairly certain there's no humor behind it. "He asked me what I knew about the drug issue. Wanted to know what Henri still owed." I don't like the sound of that or where this might be going. "He wanted to know what your plans were going forward to clear that account."

This is exactly what I was afraid of. And once Alain scents blood, there's no deterring him.

"And?"

Teague's expression turns hard and he shifts uncomfortably. Resting his elbow on the arm of the chair, he rubs his palm down his face and huffs out a sharp breath. "He asked if there would be two girls up on the auction block, if it was a buy one, get one free deal." His grip on his phone is tight enough to make his knuckles turn white. I wouldn't be surprised if the case yields under the pressure.

My pulse races, thundering through my veins. My head pounds at the added pressure. I don't know what I wanted to hear, but that was not it. "Jesus."

"Yeah." Another huff from Teague and then he bites out, "Not happening."

His obsession with the *petite femme tranquille* isn't something I understand, but I don't need to. He feels the way he feels and has held her close since we picked the girls up from the cemetery, but my gut tells me whatever is going on between them is rooted in history far deeper than what the past handful of days could hold.

Silence swirls thick between us.

At no point since pressing the plungers on her

parents did I think any old feelings would resurface toward Winnie. I really thought my anger would sustain me. The vulnerability those feelings expose is concerning.

Alain thrives off the suffering of others, doesn't matter who they are, how long he's known them or whether they're relatives. If he smells a hint of fear or the possibility of it, he's going to pop his proverbial popcorn and sit back to enjoy the show.

I want to believe that I was able to shield Winnie at dinner, but I know better.

He took notice.

Of her.

Of me.

Of the way I kept hold of her.

And now he wants both of the girls. Greedy fucking bastard.

"Christophe," Teague says, his voice low as if the walls have ears.

They have in the past but, aside from my driver whom Alain insists on remaining in my service, I cleared house. The only men I have on my team and in my employ are those I trust.

I meet his dark gaze.

"She is not to be touched. I won't stand for it. If that's going to be a problem, tell me now. I'll send her away where no one can find her." He's unnaturally still, like a big lethal cat waiting to pounce. "Give me time to make the arrangements, and then I'm yours. You know this, yeah? I've got your six and will do whatever you need me to, but let me make her safe."

I flex my jaw, the muscles bouncing with each hard grind of my teeth, and offer him a tight nod. "Do what you have to do. Put your mind at ease, but in two days we have a show to put on."

Alain won't wait any longer than that for his cash.

The wheels are already in motion and the invitations have been issued. Plans are well underway and there is no turning back now. Not that that was ever really an option, but time and distance have a habit of fucking with a person's memories.

And to say I've been fucked is like stating that water is wet.

"And you? What are you going to do about his"—he tilts his head from side to side, searching for the right word—"interest?"

Isn't that the fucking question. "I don't know." Simply put, there are not a whole lot of options.

"You could step up, demand your rightful place at the table."

This is a conversation we've had on more than one

occasion. Teague has always been in my corner, always had my back even when I had nothing but the hint of legacy within *Les Millieu*. But my uncle is all the family I have.

If my parents hadn't been slaughtered in the bloodiest of ways, things would be different. An iota of support, having even *Maman*, who stayed clear of the family's business, as counsel, a voice of reason, would have made all the difference in the world.

I was barely a man, grieving the murder of my parents. Stuck between throwing myself into a position of responsibility I was in no way ready for and doing what other kids my age were doing—going to college. Who knew a business degree would translate to mafia life, but *Les Millieu* is a business with profits and losses, our product might be different but we most definitely were a business.

"Timing is an issue," I mumble.

"Timing. You think there's ever going to be a good time to tell Alain to fuck off? You think he's going to be receptive if you ply him with—what? Winnie? A beautiful young thing for him to taunt and tease, torture and ultimately destroy?" The glare I send him doesn't seem to faze him in the least. "He's not going to willingly step down. He's not going to pat you on the back and thank you for allowing him the opportunity to hold things together until you were ready to step up and take your rightful place.

"You're going to have to overthrow the dictator, Christophe. You have your people in place, ready and willing to back you in this coupe, but you have to want it." There's not another man alive who could talk to me the way Teague does. He's the only one who can get away with laying it all out there for me, and he knows that.

That doesn't stop the warning glare I shoot him. "I do want it," I growl.

"But...?"

I sigh. But is right. What's holding me back? Fear of the unknown? Fear of the known? Because I have no doubt if I go straight for his throat, Alain will put me down like a dog.

"It's late," I deflect. "Tomorrow, we make a plan."

Teague stiffens, pulling back from me. "I have shit of my own to take care of tomorrow. You gave me two days. I'm going to need them to—"

"Tomorrow, we plan. Then we each take care of business and reconvene prior to the event, but I'm done talking tonight." I push back from my desk and stand, draining my whiskey before depositing the empty crystal to the table just inside the door. "Get some sleep; it might be the last you have for a while," I tell him.

I stalk from the room, leaving Teague alone in my office. If he wants to waste his time sitting in there wondering what the fuck the next few days will bring, that's his prerogative. I have things I need to sort out on my own before our joint planning session.

The fewer people who know what's going to go down, the better.

I only get one shot at this; I can't fuck it up.

Chapter 15

Derailed

Winnie

Morning comes after what feels like not a single minute of restful sleep. Did I fall asleep eventually after my brain and heart chased each other from one thought to the next? Sure. Probably. Maybe a little, but not near enough to execute the half-assed plan I came up with between tossing and turning.

Watery sunlight filters through the windows as if taunting me in my plush prison. Whatever sunlight and positive boost the weather is willing to give me today matters.

After showering, I dig through the wardrobe, carefully picking pieces made for movement. Leggings and a soft long sleeved shirt under a hoodie is the best I manage to come up with. I grab an extra hoodie, leggings, and a handful of socks.

Are my feet cold? No, not at all, but there are no shoes in my wardrobe. None. The strappy stilettos Garrick set out for me to wear to dinner have been removed. The shoes I wore graveside have disappeared.

My best guess is that it's intentional. In theory, it makes it harder for me to run without shoes. Pffft, they don't know me if they think that little detail will hold me down.

The door swings open as I finish pulling on my socks, admitting Garrick and his usual tray full of food. I shove the extra leggings under a throw pillow and lean back against it.

"Good morning, miss. I trust you slept well?" he asks, a brow hiked high as he notes the dark circles under my eyes. "Perhaps after breakfast, you'll enjoy a nap."

"That was the kindest *You look like shit, Winnie* I've ever heard." I allow a smile to pull at my lips.

"I'm terribly sorry, miss. It was not my intent to offend—"

My laugh cuts him off. "Sometimes the truth hurts; it's totally fine."

He sets the tray down and reaches for the silver cloche when I stall his actions this time.

"Do you think I could have breakfast with Tru? I

missed her last night." I need her close if there's going to be any chance at all of my plan working.

He sets the silver dome back in place and straightens, adding, "I believe that can be arranged. Would you like to accompany me to her suite, or shall I bring her here?"

I burrow further into the corner of the settee and stifle a fake yawn. "Do you mind bringing her here?"

"Not at all. I'll return shortly with Miss Cochonette." He nods and steps out into the hall, the telltale scrape of the lock sliding into place punctuating his exit.

As soon as his footsteps fade away, I hop up and dart back to the bedroom to grab another hoodie for Tru. I tuck three pairs of socks in the front pocket; it's all I have. I harbor no doubt that if we manage to get out of here, our feet will be torn up by the time we get even halfway through the woods.

When I return to the sitting room, Tru is there, standing in the center of the room with her hands tucked up in the sleeves of her soft pink cardigan. Her face is relaxed, her eyes clear. I haven't seen her look this good in ages, and it bothers me that she seems better here. I don't like it.

"Where's Garrick?" I approach her slowly, keeping my tone light.

She turns to face me. "He w-went to get my b-b-breakfast."

I don't know exactly how much time that gives us, but I need to move fast so we're ready to go.

"Here"—I hand her the hoodie bunched in my hand—"Put this on over your sweater. When Garrick gets back, we're going to rush him and run."

Her brows drop. "W-w-w-we're w-w-what?" She struggles to set the words free, the sudden change of plans amping up her anxiety.

I reach into the floor lamp in the corner and unscrew the bulb, cracking the fragile glass into the huge blue and white vase that's probably a priceless antique from another time and place. Sadly, it's about the only thing available to try to knock someone out so we can run.

With the lightbulb socket tucked in the front pocket of my hoodie, I set the vase next to the door and turn to face Tru.

"Okay sweets, I need you to be strong for me. We have to work together and move fast, cool?" The timid nod is maybe the best I can hope for from her. "This isn't going to be easy, but we have to try to get out of here." I run down my plan, keeping things as simple and concise as I can so I don't overwhelm her any more than necessary.

Eyes wide, she stammers, "B-b-b-but—"

"No *buts*, Tru, we've got to go. You ready?"

She nods just as the lock slides, and the door swings open.

I heft the vase high and swing with everything I have, hitting Garrick hard enough that he goes down in a clatter of food and dishes. It's louder than I thought it would be, but this is probably a poorly thought out plan at the very best.

"Tru, hand me those." I point to where I set the leggings on the arm of the settee and, as efficiently as I can, tie the butler's hands behind his back. It's not great, but it's going to have to do.

I peer out into the hallway. There's not a soul in sight so I turn for Tru, finding her standing over Garrick with sadness pinching at her eyes.

"We need to go. Stick close to me and be as quiet as you can," I whisper, grabbing her hand and pulling her along behind me.

With my head on a swivel, I lead her down the long hallway counting our lucky stars that no one is rushing to see what the crashing commotion was all about. Maybe the tray flying wasn't near as loud as it seemed to me?

The French doors that lead out to the stone paved patio at the back of the house are mere steps away. I pause and whisper, "When we get through the doors, run like the devil is chasing you, Tru. Go straight for the woods and we'll find our way home, got it?"

Her grip on my hand tightens and I can only hope that's her silent understanding.

When I try to free my hand, she squeezes even harder.

"It'll be okay, just let me get this door open and I'll hold your hand while we run, I promise." The last thing I want to do is release the makeshift weapon in my pocket but Tru is not letting up on her grip at all. "Tru, let go." I twist to look at her and am met with an expression somewhere between adoration and fear.

Unease bubbles in my belly as I follow her line of sight only to find not one, but two tall, broad walls of pissed off men stalking toward us. And when she releases me, her hand slipping from mine, I want nothing more than to snatch it back.

I fumble with the lock on the French doors and push them wide. In a flail of hands that would be comical if our lives weren't on the line, I finally grab hold of her hand and drag her outside with me.

Our feet no sooner hit the flagstones, than her hand is ripped from mine like she wasn't even trying to stick with me. In fact, she's standing on her own, turning toward Teague as if they're magnets and she's drawn to him.

"Tru!" Her name bursts from me full of panic.

She doesn't spare me a glance until she's locked within the prison of her captor's arms. He lowers his lips to murmur something soft and lilting, a poem and a promise, against the shell of her ear. The soft smile she has for him battles with the pleading eyes she turns in my direction.

A battle rages inside me. Do I stay and try to drag her away from the man whose arms she willingly fell into? Or do I run, try to get myself to safety and then figure out how to come back for her?

Ultimately, it doesn't matter.

Any decision is snatched away as Teague turns them and spirits her away from the growing tension.

A strong hand wraps around my wrist, holding me in place. In a burst of something I can't even begin to name, I wrench my pitiful weapon from my pocket and slash it through the air toward Christophe, catching on his chest.

Bright red blooms, staining the front of his crisp white shirt. The blood spreads creating a work of abstract art on the pristine white canvas of fine linen. It would be beautiful if not for the fact that I likely just sealed my fate—or made it a whole lot worse.

Short, sharp breaths punctuate my wasted efforts to get free.

Christophe pulls me close, banding his arm around

my lower back while maintaining hold of my wrist. I wriggle and strain, trying to put enough space between us to drive my knee into his crotch, but I can't.

I lash out with my free hand, but he stops me again, grabbing that hand mid-strike and locking it behind my back with the other. There's no way I can escape the hold he has on me.

Christophe wrenches the socket from my grip and tosses it away. "Didn't know honeybees could sting," he growls, swiping his hand through the crimson stain over the spot his heart should be because it's obvious he no longer has one. He captures my jaw in his palm, smearing the blood down my neck until he finds my racing pulse. Then he squeezes.

Panic rips through me as I imagine him crushing the life out of me.

"Be careful, honeybee. You may have drawn blood first, but I promise you don't want me to do the same to you. The blood I want to see, is blood you can't afford."

The words tumble from his lips in a haze as the edges of my vision pull in and the world goes dark.

Consciousness seeps back in as I'm laid gently on my bed. Christophe looms over me, fists planted firmly on the mattress to either side of my head.

"There she is," he says as my eyes pop open. "What were you thinking, *chéré?* Did you really think you could get away? That I wouldn't see you? There are cameras—"

"Everywhere, Garrick told me," I croak. As soon as his name passes my lips I try to sit up only to fall back into the plush pillows when the cage of Christophe's arms keep me from moving. "Garrick...is he okay?"

"Pissed off like a bear who got his paw stuck in the beehive, but he'll be fine." He stands to his full height putting space between us.

In a really weird turn of events, I find I don't like it. How crazy is it that I felt safe, almost protected, with Christophe's heat swirling around me?

Chapter 16

Disappointment

Winnie

eighteen years old

AND JUST LIKE THAT, MY HIGH SCHOOL GRADUATION was added to that long list of life experiences blown off by my parents in the name of business.

More like drugs, sex, and money. But those were the tenets of their business, so...

The thing that made this one so hard to swallow was the absence of my best friend, my ride or die. Though seeing as how she had, in fact, almost died, I struggled with that particular phrase now.

Tru and I had been all set, our plans were solid and

ready to be set in motion, until she disappeared without a trace.

Guilt nipped at my heels because I should have known something was off, that things weren't right.

If I had been paying closer attention, I would've noticed the changes in her, in everything around us, really. But most of the changes were so small, too subtle.

Big changes happened when my father stopped having me meet his *friends* in the alley behind his club. That was the first and last time I argued with my father in public. For the most part, I didn't bother arguing with him in private after that either.

The meetings—drops, really—became much more involved after that one. They went from scary, back alley exchanges that my father sent me to all alone, to being accompanied by one of his most trusted men. The only part of it that made me feel remotely safer was that they happened behind the closed doors of a select few high-class hotels and mostly during daylight hours.

Looking at the whole thing objectively, was it really any better to meet strange men in hotel suites? It was hard to say, but the change mattered to me.

Tru didn't like it, though. She didn't like that she went from having my back and manning the getaway car, to being relegated to the sidelines.

We fought about the whole thing more than once.

Shit, we fought about it a lot. Tru didn't trust my dad to put my safety first, rightfully so, but it scared me when she started following me.

At first, I just felt like I was being watched, I didn't know it was Tru. I never thought for a minute that she was all that sneaky, but I felt eyes on me way before I eventually saw her parked across the street of the hotel downtown.

After that, the little hairs on the back of my neck prickled with awareness. And each time I had another meeting, those prickles got spicier, my shoulders filled with more and more tension.

When she disappeared, I expected the feeling to stop, but it never did. That prickly, itchy awareness became so familiar, it gave me a certain amount of peace. Security.

But Tru was gone. She disappeared without a trace.

Her father acted like nothing happened. He just waved me off with a mumbled proclamation that she was probably with her mother.

There wasn't an ounce of truth in his claims, though. My best friend wouldn't leave without me. We had a plan. We were leaving together...

I peeled the shiny polyester graduation robe from my sweaty skin and folded it as neatly as I could. It had to be returned to the school office because I didn't have the extra cash to cover the outrageous fee. Sure, other parents foot the bill for their kids who were posing for pictures with their besties, making plans for college. They'd be the ones party hopping later that night, going from house to house and celebrating as high school grads do.

Not me, though. I handed in my graduation gown and started my lonely walk home.

Not home...to the woods.

Even after all the time that had passed, it was still my safe space. And every time I turned the corner on the trail to our tree, I couldn't help but look for Christophe.

He was never there.

He'd disappeared from my life just like Tru. Little by little, piece by piece, everyone took off leaving me in their rearview mirror. Everyone except my parents. They just used me to make their lives easier.

I settled on the fallen log, deep in the woods that separated my house from Christophe's. Really, the woods separated our worlds.

How many times had he invited me to his house? How many times had he invited me into his world? To meet his mother? To have my wounds bandaged, my emotions soothed? To experience what life entailed on the other side of the tree line?

And I never went.

Fear controlled me, keeping me from experiencing the world. And it wasn't always fear of getting in trouble or fear for my safety—even as a little kid, I knew safety wasn't something I had at home. No, it was the dread of finding out that life was better literally anywhere else. At six-, ten-...even twelve years old, *that* was too scary. Far too intimidating a thought to process.

Now though, at eighteen, I would jump at the chance. I quite literally had nothing and no one left here. If it weren't for the constant, low key feeling of dread that simmered around all thoughts of Tru, I'd run. I'd go all the way around the world—to the exact spot where one step further would become a single step back in this direction.

My shoulders drooped under the weight of all the unknowns hanging over my head. I had a shit past, absolutely no plans for my future, not without Tru. I was depending on her. I needed her to get away, she was an integral part of our plan.

She took care of me.

She kept me sane

And now, I was completely alone.

I pushed myself up off the log, drawn to the large oak that held all of my dreams. The rough point of the heart I'd carved around my initials and Christophe's points to a small opening in the trunk that cradled my journal and the cash Tru and I managed to save. It wasn't nearly enough but even that small amount had been hard for us to come by—no one in town was willing to hire me.

Not even the diner wanted to give me a job waiting tables. I'd been in tears and almost crashed into a tall red-headed man in a suit as I left, feeling overwhelmed and utterly defeated. I still don't know why the owner changed his mind, but when he caught up to me at the end of the block and told me he'd reconsidered, the tears flowed just the same, but my relief was very real.

Still, getting out of here didn't look quite the same.

With nothing else to do, I opened my journal and quickly counted our cash.

I counted it again.

And then I counted it a third time, because the amount tucked between the pages was not the pittance that'd been there last time I'd checked. And in a wild twist...it wasn't less. It was enough for me to leave.

Thousands.

I slapped my hands over the crisp hundred-dollar bills and spun my head around. There was no one lurking in the trees, no one stepped into my clearing, but my heart thundered in my chest anyway.

I'd been careful, so careful, each time I went out

there. Who would have followed me? Who would have watched as I tucked my tips inside the cover of my journal?

I huffed a laugh.

Who would do all of that and then add twenty brand new, crisp hundred-dollar bills to my escape funds?

A ghost.

The ghost of my first foolish crush.

He was the only person I could think of who might've had money like that, but it made no sense. Christophe had left.

I hadn't seen him, hadn't heard from him, in almost six years, there was no way he would do something like this. Would he?

There was absolutely no way I could leave that much cash out here. My tree was solid, but it wasn't a bank. Carefully, I folded the bills and shoved them deep into my pocket, before tucking my journal back into its hiding spot.

With a final sweep of the area, I made my way back through the woods to pack up what I could. It wouldn't be much, but it wasn't like I had all that much anyway.

This would be good. This is what I'd wanted. What I'd planned...just not how.

But I could go, get set up in a cheap apartment, just

like I would have if Tru were still here, and then I'd try to figure out what had happened to her, where she'd been, and how to get her back.

What I hadn't expected to find propped up against my door was a broken and battered Tru.

Chapter 17

Delicate

Christophe

Sitting in my office, staying away from Winnie, has become a much harder challenge than I could have imagined.

She's like my own personal drug, formulated for my distinct chemical makeup.

My eyes are constantly pulled back to her image on the screen.

My focus is shit.

And I have a stupid amount of shit to take care of today. Hell, my list couldn't be any longer, and with Teague off knocking things off his own list, I'm on my own. He's the only other person I trust with tasks of a nature this sensitive.

Though I try to fight it, my gaze lands on the security monitor yet again.

Winnie is pacing, pacing, pacing, like a caged bear. Ironic comparison considering how slight she is, almost fragile in her build. Can't imagine too many times the word *delicate* is used to describe bears, but here we are. My own personal delicate bear, longing to break free of her cage while it protects her from things darker, much, much worse than me.

I hit the button on the ancient intercom on my desk and wait.

There is no way I'm going to be able to get anything done with the temptation of Winnie on my screen, and I'm not willing to turn the monitor off unless I know someone else has eyes on her. Not after her stunt yesterday. Why she thought she could escape undetected is beyond me.

I turn before even the slightest sound registers, lounging back in my chair as I address Garrick. "I need you to entertain Winnie today. Keep her busy. Distracted." It's probably the softest order I've ever issued.

"Sir?"

This is so fucking dumb, this whole thing. I heave out a heavy breath as my gaze crawls to him. Brows knit in confusion. Stiff posture. One foot slightly behind the other. He looks like he's ready to run, but I'm not entirely convinced it's from me or toward her.

"How're you feeling?" I ask, not at all surprised as confusion shifts to insult. "Your head. You got hit pretty hard last night, and—"

"I assure you, I'm perfectly fine," he grumbles.

Of course, I know that already. First thing I did was call Dr. Hibou to check Garrick out. Honestly, I was shocked that the man wasn't even concussed. A good knot on the back of his head and a severely bruised ego, but that's it.

"Right. So go hang out with Winnie today. Relax, watch a movie, read a book. Hell, grab a bottle of whiskey and get her drunk." I clench my jaw, the muscle popping, as I think over my plan for the following night. "Let her have a day before it all goes to shit."

Without a word, Garrick boldly stalks across the room to my liquor cabinet. He pops open the door and peruses the options. It's all good, highly sought after bottles that any whiskey connoisseur would love to get their hands on. But he pushes those bottles to the side and reaches past them to where I stash my special reserve.

Two bottles of high-proof, smooth as velvet whiskey are tucked in the crook of his arm, a pair of cut crystal tumblers secured in one palm. That should have them both on their asses feeling no pain. At least not today, tomorrow...that's a whole different story.

"Watch your back. She's dangerous with the good crystal," I mutter.

Garrick executes an abrupt turn with nothing short of military precision and says, "Sir, if I may speak frankly."

I suffer no fools and don't take shit from anyone, but Teague and Garrick are free to say what they need. I nod. "Go ahead."

He relaxes his stance, just slightly but enough to indicate he's got serious concerns.

"It is not my place to question your motives, sir, but where Miss L'Ourson is concerned, I would hope you might show some kindness. Perhaps a measure of forgiveness?" The scowl that mars my features does nothing to stop his lobbying. "As I understand, Miss L'Ourson has had quite the unfortunate...life, one could say. I'm not sure if you're aware of the hardships she's endured in her short life, but I implore you, sir, to recon-sider your plans regarding her and the dreadful situation her parents left her in."

A dark laugh bursts free from me.

I tried to hold it back, but honestly, there was no way I was keeping that down.

Garrick, though, he looks nothing short of personally

offended by my outburst. And if I'm asking a favor of him, I need to give him *something*.

I clear my throat and sit forward, resting my forearms on the smooth surface of my desk. "You're right"—his brows rise, hovering dangerously close to his hairline—"it's not your place. But I am well aware of the shit Winnie dealt with as a kid. Her parents were vile human beings who didn't deserve—" I stuff down my rant because while I need to give Garrick something to appease him, now is not the time for me to show my whole ass where Winnie is concerned.

"Sir?"

"I know her history and will take that into consideration. Is that what you're looking for? Feel better?"

He nods, the barest hint of a smile tugs at his lips. "Thank you, sir. Much better." He turns and strides to the door, arms laden with his spoils from my office. Again, the list of people who can get away with shit like this is wildly small.

"Garrick"—I wait for him to pause before speaking again—"make sure her day is as good as it can be."

His eyes lose their edge and his smile softens. "That will be my honor, sir."

Alone again, I slump back into my chair and stare at his retreating form. I would give just about anything to trade places with him. To spend the day with her in any way. To make up for years and years of avoidance. This distance is a necessary evil and not at all what I want, but right now, need has to come before wants and desires.

This just goes up on the scoreboard of life with all the other times I've pulled strings from deep in the wings in order to keep things from completely crumbling around her. From the very start, the first time I followed that small child through the woods to make sure she got home okay, I knew her life was shit.

There was no doubt that our lives couldn't be more different, but I did what I could. Food when she had none. Clothes when she needed them. Hell, I had her student account funded from the moment I was able. The catch was always doing it without drawing attention to her. And keeping myself far, far from view.

Was it ironic that the brutal murder of my parents was the driving force behind all of that? It was.

I had a lot to learn, but I knew I had to push her away to keep her safe.

Is it even more ironic that pushing the plunger on her parents and removing them from her life is the culmination of years of holding her at arm's length, denying her existence? Yeah, I guess it is. Nothing like killing the negligent assholes who made her life hell just to have a reason to pull her close. Not just close,

Winnie's under my skin in the best and worst ways possible.

It's been years of games and bullshit and wearing my disinterest like a mask to keep her away from this life, in the hell that she knew, before I could strategically bring her into mine.

Now, the devil is in the details, and I have precious little time to orchestrate the finale.

Each time I spare a glance to the security monitor, Winnie and Garrick are settling into their day more and more. Much as that is exactly what I need to get my shit done, what I want is to be the one sharing that bottle of whiskey with her, to see her face light up, hear her laughter. To be that fucking carefree with her? That's what I want.

If all goes to plan, that's our future.

So I put my head down and get to work confirming attendees for the auction's accelerated timeline. Validating the bidding system and wire transfer portal. Touching base with security.

Out of all the tasks I have to get through, that's the one that gives me heartburn. That's the one I need Teague for and he's off with little Miss Anxiety playing house or maybe he got her settled far from this shit show and is fucking her into a boneless, tantric, Zen, whatever the fuck state.

When he pushes into my office a couple hours later, looking rough and thoroughly fucked, my low level pissed off ramps up to fully irate.

"Nice," I grumble, tossing him a glare that would stop most men in their tracks. "Your idea of a quick out and back is far different from mine." I push back from my desk and stand. Everything tightened up while I sat at my desk doing shit I much prefer to hand off to others.

Teague sinks into the corner of the sofa on the far side of the room. He looks like absolute dogshit.

He meets my glare with one of his own. "Yeah, there was nothing quick or easy about that."

"But you have her tucked away. Safe at one of your properties?" I pour myself a whiskey and offer one to my friend. "Think you've got it in you to get some actual work done or do you need to recover from your *liaison*, your *aventure?*"

Teague's glare relaxes into an eye roll that any teenage girl would be proud of. "I wish."

I huff a laugh. "If you weren't getting your dick wet, what the fuck took you so long? The plan was to drop her off and get your ass back here, not to take a fucking personal day to—"

"Again, I fucking wish." He reaches for his laptop on the side table, pulling it to his knees before popping the lid open. He taps at the keys, his eyes darting across the screen until he seems satisfied with what he sees.

My brows push together as the glass of whiskey stalls on its way to my mouth.

"I took her to the safe house. Arranged for it to be fully stocked, everything Truie could possibly need was there, waiting for her. I had her inside, gave her the tour and had her settled. But when I moved to leave, she fucking fell apart."

"Jesus, you've gotten soft," I say.

Teague scowls and shakes his head. "The hell I have, she fought me like her life depended on it. Lashing out, hitting me, arms flailing, the whole nine yards. I assure you, Tru did not hold back, not that she inflicted much damage," he adds quickly before continuing. "The closest she got to taking me out was when she grazed my balls trying to knee me in the junk."

I can't help but laugh at the mental image of that tiny, trembly woman getting the jump on Teague.

"Go ahead and laugh, asshole. I wasted an entire day and ended up right back where we started it."

"We?"

Teague sighs, dropping his head back against the cushion of the sofa. "Yeah, we. I ended up having to bring her back here, tuck her away in my room."

Sometimes saying nothing, not asking a single question, is the best way to get straight to the information I want. And I'm sick of wasting time today. We still have a lot of shit to cover before tomorrow, and Teague's escapades have cost us valuable time.

"It was the only place she would calm down enough for me to leave her."

"So you have a woman tucked between your sheets. Good enough motivation to get this done." I drop down into my chair and drain my glass, wishing I had the same.

Chapter 18

Dominoes

Winnie

Two days.

Two days that I've been held captive in this...this luxury prison.

Two days of pampering and panicking, fighting to flee and failing miserably.

Two days of playing mental reels of the worst-case scenario for what I'm going to have to face at the auction.

And then what?

Christophe is cold, hard—in so many ways—and acts like he doesn't care, but I felt something after that dinner when he held me tight against him.

I felt more when he caught me trying to escape.

I mean, I felt a lot of things: power rolling off of him,

muscles twitching where my fingers skated over him. And his cock. I couldn't help but to feel that pressed against my stomach. With all the things he said to me—the threats, or maybe promises—of what his uncle will do if he wins me, my focus was firmly on Christophe. What he could do to me. With me.

Instead of falling into those *what-ifs* and losing myself in delicious fantasies of Christophe, I got to spend yesterday with the man whose head I tried to bash in. That was freaking awkward as shit. And when I asked to see Tru, if she could come to my room and hang out with me, Garrick just poured me another whiskey and steered the conversation far, far away from her.

Thinking back, he was obviously there to distract me. Or maybe it was punishment for letting me get one over on him, if you can call the broken vase and lump on his head that.

All I know is I had a super chill day when it should have been anything but.

Then, as soon as I was alone behind the locked door to my suite, I crawled between my sheets, shoved my hand between my legs, and tried to make myself come. *Tried.*

Maybe it was because of how drunk I was, maybe because now that I've been ruined by Christophe's touch, mine pales in comparison—I don't know—but a failed orgasm in my time of need did me in. And now, nursing a serious hangover after a restless night, I'm on edge.

Self-induced releases are nothing like the magic Christophe is capable of.

I ache.

I throb between my legs.

I've done nothing but pace and fret and try, try, try to relieve the tension buzzing through me.

There's literally nothing I can do in this lush prison to alleviate this...this...misery.

Every step highlights the need in my core.

Every thought spirals pain through my head.

The door opens, startling me, pulling me from the lascivious thoughts of just exactly where I want to trail my tongue across my captor, tasting him. And where I want to beg for his tongue to glide across me.

I whip my head around to find Garrick, looking considerably less hungover than I feel, stepping into my room once again. *My room.* When the hell did these become my rooms? When did I stop dreaming of how to escape this house? My plotting and planning have turned from fleeing Christophe's clutches to crawling closer and losing myself to him—in him.

"Excuse me, Miss L'Ourson, Mr. Robicheaux has requested your presence in his office." The butler's smile is tight, his hands clutched in front of him as though it's taking considerable effort to keep from wringing them. He looks nervous, or maybe unhappy, shifting his gaze around the room, never quite meeting mine.

"Am I in trouble again?" I don't bother trying to keep the sass from my voice. I'm wound tight and there's only so much I can keep locked down at one time.

His eyes wrinkle and a small smile pulls at the corner of his mouth. "Not that I know of, miss. But he did request I escort you to him right away." He takes a step toward the door and pulls it open.

I glance down at the leggings and wrap shirt I threw on when I dragged myself out of bed. My hair is up in a messy bun and I'm not wearing a stitch of makeup. Why my appearance concerns me, I'd rather not spend too much time or effort examining. I don't need to face that kind of introspection today. Or ever, maybe.

"Do I need to 'dress' for this meeting?" I air-quote the shit out of that, joining Garrick as he chuckles and shakes his head.

"Not at all." He sweeps his free hand toward the hallway, indicating I should go ahead of him. "You look perfect just the way you are." He's so sweet. Wrong in his assessment, but absolutely the sweetest.

When all is said and done—when I'm long gone after this stupid skin auction—I might actually miss him.

We walk side-by-side to Christophe's office. Garrick allows me to enter first and then softly grasps my elbow, halting my progress. "It has been a pleasure, Miss L'Ourson. I wish you"—his eyes cloud and he clears his throat—"I wish you all the best." The last bit comes with a harsh glare toward Christophe. It seems as though Garrick is less than thrilled with his boss.

I throw my arms around the kind man, comforted when his hand rests on the center of my back and he pulls me close. He's been nothing but kind to me. Almost fatherly in the time I've spent under this roof, other than the part where he's delivered me to Christophe time and time again but maybe bashing him over the head balances those transgressions out.

I step into the office, images of the last time we were in here together crashing through my mind. My heart stutters in my chest and desire swirls in my core, tightening my belly. A laugh bubbles up from there and gets stuck in my throat.

Christophe is beautiful. He's powerful and electric. But he is not the same boy I fell for all those years ago. He's selling my body to the highest bidder to—what?—impress his uncle? Stay in that vile man's good graces?

Even knowing that, I can't shake this overwhelming desire I have for him. I hate the fact that I want him.

What I want doesn't matter.

What my body is begging for is inconsequential.

And my heart? That stupid muscle can fuck right off, because who in their right mind would have any room in their heart for someone who can treat them so callously, hurt them so easily? How can it beat for him as he tosses it aside without a care? Tosses it aside and stomps on it. Shreds it.

He always has and from the way things are going, he always will.

Christophe might want to fuck me, but he has never had a problem walking away from me and I don't see any hints of that changing. Certainly not now.

Not when he's so focused on the money my parents owed him.

Not when he reminds me of how much my virginity will sell for, while he's got his hand in my pants strumming me until I'm quivering like a newborn woodland animal trying to stand for the first time.

He takes me in from head to toe. His gaze caresses me, the heat in his eyes burning me as he lingers on my hips and thighs, my chest and neck, my mouth. His silence is complete and if I'm honest, completely unnerving.

I shift under his perusal.

"You uncomfortable with this, honeybee? The way I look at you?"

I still. "No."

A dark chuckle rumbles from deep in his chest. "No? The blush painting your creamy skin says something very different." He circles me slowly, pausing behind me before stepping back in front of me, arms crossed, chin tilted down. Eyes dark.

I clear the nerves from my throat. "Why am I here?" I wish I had taken a moment to clear my throat a second time, given myself a pep-talk, because that question doesn't come out with near enough confidence.

"It's time," he says.

"For?"

Another low laugh. "Time to get you ready for your big night on stage."

My brows pinch together. "But the auction is next week. You said—"

"And now it's tonight." He reaches out, running his thumb along my bottom lip.

I'm tempted to wrap my lips around the tip and pull it into my mouth, suck on it, twirl my tongue around it— lure him in and then sink my teeth in and bite the fucker.

"After your stunts earlier this week, I think it's best for me to supervise your preparations."

"You're shitting me," I say, wide-eyed. Why am I

shocked? Why does the loss of yet another illusion of control surprise me?

At the tug of his lips into a sardonic grin, my shoulders deflate. Not just my shoulders…every last bit of me. I have nothing left in me to fight him. I'm exhausted.

"Okay." I roll my lips between my teeth and nod, lifting my gaze to meet his. "Okay. Is someone meeting me in my room?"

He stares at me for so long, I wonder if he's going to bother responding.

"How much time do I have to get ready?" I ask as I walk toward the open door of the office.

I mumble "excuse me" to the huge man blocking the way. The man who looks at Tru with softness, such tenderness, stares at me like I'm nothing more than a commodity.

Christophe huffs a laugh behind me drawing the man's attention from me. "Teague, you brought everything?"

"Yeah, boss." He moves into the room, herding me back with every step.

I have no choice but to get out of Teague's way or get run over by him and I'm not about to let that happen. I may not have much—even my dignity is dwindling by the minute—but I will do whatever I can to not stumble and fall on my ass. Again.

Christophe's goon stalks across the room and deposits a small black carry-on case next to a chair set in front of a massive mirror propped in the corner. He hangs a garment bag from the mirror's frame, and retreats to the door.

"Anything else, boss?"

Christophe dismisses him with a chin lift adding, "Do what you need and be ready to leave when we're through in here."

Aside from a grunt, there's no response, just the near-silent click of the door closing me in here with Christophe.

"What is this?" I glance at the case and garment bag.

"Shit, you need to get yourself ready." Christophe settles into a club chair, stacking his ankle on the opposite knee.

I huff out a laugh, hands propped on my hips. "You had your dude pack up the stuff from my room and bring it down here?"

"I did."

He can't mean for me to get ready here—in his office.

"What if he forgot something?"

"Everything is there," he says, focused on his phone.

"And—what?—you're just going to sit there and watch?"

He lifts his gaze, spearing me with it.

I wish he'd go back to staring at his phone.

I wish he'd let me go back to my room.

I wish he'd just let me go.

"You need to be supervised." He repeats his earlier statement but slower, enunciating each word like I don't understand them.

I'm not an idiot; I understand the words, just not the implication behind them.

I cross my arms over my chest and narrow my eyes at him.

It doesn't take long for tension to swirl thick between us.

The way Christophe arches his brow at me, his lush bottom lip pinched between his forefinger and thumb, doesn't help to dissipate that tension, and I shift, rubbing my thighs together to try and alleviate desire pooling in my core.

I don't want to be turned on. I want to be pissed. I want to scream and yell and rage. I want to slap that smug, sensual, beautiful look off his sexy face.

Tears sting my eyes, threatening to spill over and slide down my face. But I don't want to show him anything—no frustration, no emotion, nothing. I blink rapidly, gnawing on the inside of my lip. Anything to stall and try to compose myself.

After a shaky exhale I ask, "Are there requirements? Anything I need to pay particular attention to?"

I know I screwed up by not even trying at dinner the other night, but I'm not the girliest of girls. I do okay with makeup, but as a rule, I keep things simple. I've never wanted to draw attention to myself.

Christophe tilts his head, assessing me. His gaze darts to the garment bag and his lips twitch as if he's not willing to allow a smile to breach his hard exterior. He slides his tongue along his bottom lip and pulls it between his teeth. The look is carnal. Predatory. *Shit hot.*

"You've taken marketing courses, make your product as irresistible as you can. After all, you have a debt to cover."

How does he know what I've studied in school? I didn't tell him, did I?

We haven't talked about much beyond what I owe him and how he expects me to pay. But he knows things. Christophe seems to know things about me that aren't as simple as common knowledge.

I expect him to know stuff about my parents; they were the ones who worked for him. But me? That doesn't make sense.

He indicates the makeshift vanity area with a nod. "Best get to it. You've only got this one opportunity to shine. Once that pretty little cherry's been popped, you won't be nearly as valuable."

His words leave me speechless, once again on the verge of tears.

"You can't stay in this little corner of the woods waiting for opportunity to come to you. You have to put yourself together and go grab what you need by the balls."

I swallow the lump in my throat and sink into the chair.

He's right.

I have to put on my armor and prepare to shine.

Chapter 19

Determination

Christophe

I thought Winnie, braless in a tight, cropped shirt and booty shorts with her ass peeking out would be the death of me. But this...?

This version of her is so much more lethal.

Every lock of hair brushed, and curled, and coaxed into glossy golden waves. Pristine skin polished and buffed to perfection. Dark, dramatic eyes with lashes thick and black. But those lips...Her plump lips that beg to be kissed, tasted—devoured—are painted deep crimson.

She's flawless and all I want to do is mess her up. Smudge the red from her mouth—leave her lips bee-stung and swollen.

Watch her mascara run, black pooling under her eyes as she stares up at me from where she kneels between my feet.

I watched her paint it all on. Every stroke, every line. I sat in my chair, phone in hand, legs crossed, and dick hard as steel.

As if her everyday clean face and messy hair isn't enough to make me fall all over myself, each layer she applied was like a shield of armor, a cloak of confidence wrapping around her. Shoulders back. Spine ramrod straight. Sexy as fuck.

And then she dropped the last vestige of sweet, young Winnie. She unzipped the garment bag—the fucking garment bag that held a sorry excuse for a dress. More like silky straps that crisscross her body, scarcely covering her tits. Barely reaching low enough on her hips to keep her pussy from view. She's a fucking wet dream.

She stood in front of the mirror adjusting the lie of the straps, ass popping from the black stilettos, the red soles perfectly matching her dress. And her lips. And the heat burning through me.

I had to tell her twice to put the detachable skirt on for her arrival at the club. And then I still had to physically wrap it around her waist, fastening it securely.

I would love nothing more than to kill the bastard

who selected this poor excuse for a dress for her. But I'm not ready to die.

I have too much yet to do.

I step out of my town car, positioning my body strategically as Winnie emerges, to ensure no one gets a view of what they're here to fight for. We're barely out of the car and I can already feel hungry eyes clocking her every move.

Interest is at an all-time high tonight.

Even moving the auction up with no notice, has the Honey Pot filled well beyond capacity.

The Glock at my waist, Teague at our backs, and the knowledge that every single asshole inside has been stripped of whatever weapons they were stupid enough to think they could smuggle in safely is locked away only offers a marginal sense of security. I know who these people are—I grew up in the company of a good number of them—and I don't trust them in the least.

I plant my hand on Winnie's back and guide her inside where she's whisked away by the auction hostess.

"You planning on following her back there?" Teague asks. His question stops me in my tracks, and I realize I'm halfway down the wrong hallway. "We have shit to do. We need to assess the room, check the guests, and make sure we're up and running for wire transfers before this thing starts."

I pause, waiting for Winnie to disappear from sight before stalking toward the office. I don't spend much time here at the club—no time, if I can help it. The Honey Pot is not my scene, seedy and distasteful. Bad for even a strip club.

We check the guest list, the financials, and finally, the security feed. Images of the main room from various viewpoints fill the wall of monitors.

Tonight's take promises to be through the roof.

To maximize revenue, the hostess has the girls mingling with buyers prior to opening the bidding. Which is one of the reasons the event is heavily guarded by *my* people. I stand to gain tremendously tonight; I won't trust the security to anyone else's men.

Short skirts and sky-high heels are easy enough to spot in the crowded club. My eyes dart from screen to screen, scanning the faces, the bodies, for *her*.

"Whoa," Teague mumbles, standing straight and backing away from me. "You want me to get you a drink, boss?"

I'm hard pressed to rip my focus from the screen to acknowledge that he's spoken to me. "What?" I bite out.

"You look like you're about to bust through that wall and kill anyone within arm's reach of Winnie. You're not planning to let Alain actually win her, are you?" Tilting his head to activate his comms, he mumbles directions for security to step in on a buyer getting a little too hands on with one of the girls before turning his attention back to me.

"Alain?" I search the room and find him in a cloud of cigar smoke. "What the fuck is he doing here? Find out who his source is. I want them dead." Alain is the primary reason we moved the auction up a handful of days. The way he looked at Winnie as she perched on my lap had me seeing red.

I pull Teague back before he can exit the office with a question. "What else did he say to you the other night? I know there was more."

"As he was leaving? He asked me if Winnie was the virgin. If she's really untouched." His brows lower over his eyes. "He said he wanted to add her to his collection."

Alain likes them young. Likes to break them in, be the first to fuck them. Ruin them and cast them aside. His reach knows no boundaries.

"You know how he operates, Christophe. He's going to bid her up high, then let some other fucker win and pay. Have his men intercept her and the payment"—Teague pauses, eyes dropping to my clenched fists—"He'll revel in the fact that he'll get to fuck her and destroy you at the same time."

"Go. Get her off the floor," I growl. "Over my dead body."

One of Alain's men has his hand wrapped around Winnie's arm leading her across the floor and straight to the Devil himself.

I watch as my uncle, my father's twin brother, reaches out and pulls Winnie's body into his. His pudgy hand squeezes her ass, and I lose the tenuous grip on my control. "Bring her to me, *now*," I roar. "Get on comms and get one of our guys to that corner immediately, for fuck's sake."

Teague storms out of the office, hand to his ear, barking orders as he goes.

I watch the screen, unwilling to take my eyes off of what could very well become a huge shitstorm. Alain is not generally receptive to the word *no*, so it doesn't surprise me that his face sours, his hand jabbing at the air with that foul fucking cigar as he cuts his men down. One of *les beaux voyous* takes off after Teague and Winnie, but security stops him before he makes it into the hall.

"Where are you taking me?" Winnie asks Teague, her voice trembling.

Not feeling so sure of yourself at the moment, are you honeybee?

I reach for her hand, pulling her behind me to close

us into the office. Before the door clicks shut, I bark an order at Teague. "End of the hall—stay there. No one comes back here, understand?"

He nods and strides away as I slide the lock in place.

I turn slowly, trying to calm my rage before facing Winnie. It doesn't work. All I can see when I look at her is Alain's hands on her. Him touching her, squeezing her ass. The way his fingers slid beneath the useless fucking, red bands that do nothing to cover her and everything to showcase her curves, highlighting everything a man could want.

This is not how the night was supposed to go. He's not supposed to be here, and Winnie's supposed to remain untouched.

I can't imagine what she sees as her gaze skates over my face, but we are too close to the finish line to let the mask fall now.

I don't give her a chance to say a goddamn thing as I wrap my hand around her throat and walk, pushing until all she can feel is the wall at her back, and me—every hard inch of me—pressing into her.

"Did you like that old man touching you? His hands on you while he was picturing you spread out beneath him?" Her throat bobs against my palm as she swallows down her fear. "Because I didn't fucking like it. Not at all." I grind the words between my teeth.

The desire I've been suppressing over the last few days—hell, it's been years—is overwhelming. I'm riding a knife's edge of playing a role and giving those fucking *wants* free rein.

I palm her tit, pushing the scarlet scraps beneath her creamy flesh and pinch her pretty pink nipple. She gasps at the bite of pain as I do the same to her other breast.

"I need a taste," I mumble, pulling one perfect nipple into my mouth—licking, sucking, nipping—until she squirms and her breath hitches.

She's fucking perfect.

I slide my hand down her soft belly, over the flare of her hips, and cup her ass—my hand exactly where Alain's was just moments ago. I want to erase him from her. Replace each of his proprietary touches with one of my own.

I release her nipple with the scrape of my teeth and stand, my lips hover just above hers. "Who feels better pressed against you?" I ask, my mouth brushing over hers. "Who would you rather picture above you? Behind you? Spreading you out. Worshipping you. Fucking you soundly?"

"You." She breathes out her response and I greedily suck it in, swallowing it down.

I slide my hand between her legs, sweeping a finger beneath her soaking-wet thong. "You like that—the thought of my body above yours, my fat cock spearing you, stretching you wide." Every fantasy I've had of her spills from my lips. The things I want to do to her, with her. To teach her and show her pleasure she's only ever imagined.

"Yes." She tilts her hips, granting me more access.

I circle her opening with the pad of my finger, pushing, dipping in and spreading her juices.

She pants and mewls with every dip.

The sounds she makes are merely a tease; I want her moaning, writhing, gasping beneath me. I want her fingernails digging into my flesh, for her to mark me the way she fucking owns me.

I want it to be my name on her lips as I pound into her, the sound echoing through the room as she comes apart.

Maybe she knows where my thoughts are, maybe neither of us are thinking at all, because when I pump my finger into her tight cunt and then add another, spreading them, stretching her, she moans my name, her muscles squeezing, hips rocking.

I drop to my knees and replace my fingers with my tongue, delving into her silky depths and savoring the way she tastes.

The hint of her protest rolls right into cries of ecstasy. And me?—I've died and gone to heaven.

She's sweet like the purest honey.

Every swirl of my tongue around her tight little bud of nerves has her gasping and writhing in pleasure. I lick into her pussy, and suck each of her lips into my mouth, relishing everything about this moment. When she's trembling in my grasp, I wrap my lips around her clit and suck—*hard*—until her hips buck against my face, coating me in her juices. I bracket her swollen nub between my teeth teasing the tip of her clit with my tongue. The bite of pain, the overall sensation—I don't know—has her spearing her fingers through my hair. Pulling me in tight. Pushing me away.

Responsive.

Head thrown back; lips parted.

Delicious.

Legs quivering and hips rocking.

I want to devour her.

Gasping for air as she floods my tongue.

"Fuck, yes. Give it to me, honeybee. I need everything you've got." Like a man possessed, I slide three fingers inside her, pump them in and out as I feast on her, needing her to come for me. The sounds are liquid and messy and sexy as fuck. I push deeper, lost in her, consumed by my need for her.

"Stop," she gasps at the intrusion and squeezes her

thighs together trapping my hand. She pushes hard against me, shoving me with everything she has.

"Stop, Christophe. You have to stop."

She uses my surprise to rip herself away from me and escape. Her grasp on the edge of the desk is all that's holding her up because those long, beautiful legs are boneless and doing nothing for her.

I stand and face her, wiping my mouth with the back of my hand. My eyes narrow as I pin her in place. "I don't have to do a fucking thing," I warn.

A handful of steps has my dick pressed against her ass, separated by my trousers and the scrap of red silk she's trying to smooth back into place. I grab a handful of her hair and push until her chest is pressed against the desk. The thought of taking her like this, bent over and balancing on her toes, ass in the air, has me burning up.

I shove my foot between hers to kick them apart but far more agile than she should be right now, Winnie twists away from me and puts far too much space between us.

Cheeks flushed, tits heaving, and bee-stung lips, she looks like a goddess. A beautiful, messy goddess and I want to spend a lifetime worshipping her. Hell, she's the only woman I have ever gotten down on my knees for.

In the space of a heartbeat, the heat swirling between us shifts and I move.

One step and her hand flies up, palm out.

Two steps and her shoulders drop, her jaw set.

"Don't. Don't come closer."

I smirk. "I plan on coming, honeybee, but only after I get you there again. I want to hear my name fall from your lips as you come apart. I want you to scream for me."

"No." Her hands flutter across her chest, adjusting the front bands of her dress, putting herself back together.

"I agree, no." I wrap my hands around her delicate wrists and growl as I erase the space between us. "Don't you hide what's mine from me."

She inhales deep and expels the air like it's offended her.

If she wants to do this with restricted air, I'm happy to make that happen. Her throat would be so pretty with my hand wrapped around it.

I shake my head and try to make sense of her bullshit words buzzing softly against the exposed skin of my throat, but they make no sense. "What did you say?" I ask, my voice low.

"I'm not yours. I...I don't belong to you, Christophe. We can't do this." The cadence of her words is slow, measured as though she's explaining something ridiculously simple. Maybe she is.

She frees her wrists from my grasp and splays her hands out in front of her. "You said this is all I have that's worth anything. If you fu— If we do this, I have nothing. I can't pay you what you think I owe. Then what? Huh? You won't even tell me the amount of my parents' debt. I have no options, you said so yourself. This? My virginity is all I have to offer; you can't take that away from me."

Chapter 20

Desire

Winnie

"I won't let anyone else have what's mine." Christophe growls at my back as I walk out of the office, thighs shaking and slick with my orgasm.

I flinch, though I don't know if it's from what he says or from the way his claim reverberates through me.

I have to do this. I have no other options.

As I stalk down the hallway to the main room Teague rushes toward me pulling up short when he lifts his gaze from the phone clutched in his hand. His brows rise, surprise slashed across his face.

The fast-paced speech of a typical auctioneer might be missing, but there's no doubt from the buzzing energy spilling from the room beyond that the auction has begun. A single voice calls attention to each attribute of the poor girl on stage at the moment. Rude and lurid comments drift down the hallway between the call and confirmation of astronomical dollar amounts.

"Are they starting?" I ask, brushing past him.

Teague's hand engulfs my upper arm as he stops me. He stares at me, gaze darting from me to the man I know is standing behind me. "Boss?"

Glancing over my shoulder shows me Christophe framed in the doorway to the office, highlighted by weak, yellow light. His jaw shifts, eyes narrow, but he doesn't say a damn word. Not a thing until the silence is heavy and cold, pressing outward and filling the space.

Teague tilts his head listening to the buzz of words in his earpiece. His questioning gaze shoots to Christophe who nods almost imperceptibly.

"What the hell are you doing?" he asks Christophe, disbelief tainting his words. "You're going to let this happen?"

Why wouldn't he? Christophe has done nothing but tell me I owe him. That I'm on the hook for a debt I didn't accrue and one I certainly can't pay. I'm stuck.

Christophe prowls toward us, lethal promise in every measured step.

A suited security guy pops his head into the hall. "Sir, we need the girl for the next bid."

"Let her go," Christophe says. Cold. Emotionless like the primal passion from just minutes ago never happened, that it was nothing but a dream. The only hint he shows that he just had his face buried between my legs is the swipe of his thumb through the edge of his beard before he slides it between his lips.

Teague releases me, handing me off with a scowl at his boss.

Before walking away, I turn and address him. "Take care of Tru for me. Make sure she gets somewhere safe. I won't beg for myself. I won't ask you for anything else; I just need for her to be okay."

Teague stiffens at my request, only relaxing marginally when Christophe responds, "I will."

Head high, shoulders back, and spine straight, I turn my back on the first man I ever loved. All he's done is play with me—my emotions, my body. My heart. *God, the things he's made me feel.* Alive and wanted.

For all the wrong reasons? Yeah. But he's always been elusive, more an imaginary friend than anything rooted in reality.

My reality, though. That's always been the stuff of nightmares. I saw things no child should ever see. Experienced hunger and neglect and complete disregard by

the people who were supposed to love me uncondi-
tionally.

I've been taking care of myself for as long as I can
remember with only determination and a few almost mirac-
ulous finds of food or money or even clothes falling into my
lap when I needed them most. This fucked up situation isn't
all that different really. Tenacity runs through my veins,
and if a fortuitous miracle happens to make an appearance,
even better. But there's only one path for me to take.

I stalk away to face my fate.

Christophe

"What are you thinking?" Teague spits his demand.

I get it. From his perspective, I just let my life-long
obsession walk away from me and straight into a hive of
angry, buzzing hornets.

I'm not. Not really.

I couldn't live with myself if I did.

"Don't worry, brother." I turn back to the office so I
can watch the proceedings without distraction. Thank
Christ for the wall of monitors giving me every possible
view of the bidding floor.

Winnie walks out onto the stage like this is a charity
fashion show and not the vile trading of cash for pretty

little sex slaves that it is. She has no idea who the people ogling her are, what they're capable of.

They see her as nothing more than a commodity, something to be purchased and used, then discarded once she's broken. A beautiful plaything, they can't wait to sully and destroy.

I see the real Winnie. Her show of poise and grace conceals what's going on inside her. A flush spreads over her chest as she strides across the stage, her *attributes* being announced, her virginity held in the highest regard.

Those men want to use her.

"How can you say that? Look at that fucking vulture out there. You're okay with this shit?" Teague steps up next to me, gaze darting over the monitors until he finds what he's looking for. "Fucking bastard."

"Which one? The room is filled with them." I chuckle but follow his line of sight and zero in on my uncle.

Alain's eyes are glued to the stage and he's chewing on his damn cigar like he hates it. He lifts a meaty finger and nods, then does it again. And again.

I never doubted he'd bid on Winnie, given the chance. I just figured he'd wait until the end and drop an outrageous dollar amount. Instead, he's doing exactly what Teague said he would, driving the price higher and higher with every flick of his wrist.

Winnie crosses the stage again, slowly spinning at the prompt from the auctioneer, his finger twirling in the air.

Rage burns through me as every man's focus drops to her pert ass. The silk scraps do nothing to discourage their lewd thoughts or their aggressive bids.

The offers climb fast and high.

I want to blind every single one of them. Take away their sight so their vile gaze can never touch her again. And then I'll kill them. Fuck, I should go out there and claim her in front of every one of them, then lock the doors behind me and set the entire building on fire. Watch it burn to the fucking ground.

"He's doing it. He's fucking doing it," Teague grinds out, incensed.

My focus goes back to Alain to see him nod once again before shoving his cigar into his mouth and walking out of the room. Another monitor shows him leaving the building and climbing into his car. When only his retreating taillights remain on the screen, I glance back to the spot he just vacated to see one of his men remains, stance wide, arms crossed, fully focused on Winnie.

"Tell me what you know, T. What does Alain think he's doing?"

A muscle jumps in Teague's jaw, and if I didn't know better, I'd think he was enamored with Winnie too. But I know where his loyalties lie—all of them.

"He wants her, without a doubt. Put a no-cap bid on her to ensure that he's the one to take her home. You know what he's going to do to her, right? Sick fuck is going to chain her up and make her beg—"

"Stop."

"Make her beg for death, because living as his fuck doll is worse than that." He shifts uncomfortably, his hands clenched into hard fists. "Even if she manages to eventually get away, the damage will already be done."

"I know, goddamn it. I fucking know. I've seen them when he's done with them. I've seen the death and the living dead. But why Winnie? Why is he torqued over her?"

Alain's tastes are wide and varied. Girls way too young, wives and girlfriends of his enemies, and even those of his associates. His kink is destroying people by taking what's most meaningful and torturing them with it. He did it to Tru's parents. He tried to do it to my father, but he died before Alain could see it through.

Stillness falls over my friend. When he turns to face

me, he looks absolutely haunted. "You fucking know," he states.

"What do I know, Teague, tell me?"

"He wants her because of you. He wants her because she means something to you." His shoulders round and he runs a hand through his hair. "He will do anything—*everything*—to take you down. Don't you see that? You are the only thing left between him and the full power of this organization."

I laugh—not a happy one, but because he's wrong. "He already has the organization. He made sure to lock that down when my father died. Stepped in with the claim that it was just until I was older, more prepared for the role, but we've known all along that he's not going to step aside. He's proven it at every turn."

Teague scoffs. "And still, you're standing here doing nothing, knowing full and well, that he's arranged to steal Winnie away tonight."

This time my laugh is real and true.

"Teague, brother. We both knew this was a possibility, even with all the last minute changes. If you think for a minute I didn't put additional measures in place for tonight, you're sorely mistaken. I thought you had more faith in me than that."

"I do, but he's got a guy standing in the main room waiting to steal Winnie away and deliver her to his door." He gets louder with every word, strain evident in his voice. His gestures are almost wild, jerky and full of frustration.

A satisfied smile tugs at my lips. "Alain will be outbid." I glance at the monitors and then to my phone. The final bids are in, and the auction is closed. I hit the button to access volume from the auction floor.

"Gentlemen, congratulations to our winners. When your funds have been transferred and verified, you can collect your purchases. And as always, we thank you for your generosity." The auctioneer glances at the camera mounted at the back of the room and subtly adjusts his cuffs before walking off stage. The move is natural, draws no attention but conveys the message loud and clear.

"Jesus, Christophe, it's done. Alain thinks he's the high bidder. He fucking made arrangements. Did we plan for his level of sore loser?" Teague is upset. Rightfully so since he was gone for a good chunk of my planning time yesterday and is taking things at face value. But he should know that nothing—fucking nothing—is as it seems in our world.

I tuck my phone away and slide my hands into my trouser pockets as I stroll to the door. I turn and address Teague over my shoulder.

"He was never going to win her. I made damn sure of that."

Teague shakes his head. "How, though? What did you set up to cheat the motherfucker king of backstabbing cheats?"

It's more than a little annoying that he's standing here questioning my ability. I drop my head down, my chin resting on my chest for a moment before I meet his hard stare. "I'm the one who has been watching, waiting. Learning everything I could from him."

"But..."

Fists clenched at my sides, it takes a lot of effort not to knock him back into reality, but I don't have time for his bullshit. I have to go get Winnie.

"Because Winifred L'Ourson is mine. She's fucking mine. I have waited long enough for this day. To knock Alain off his fucking pedestal and take my rightful place in the organization."

"And you—what?—thought it was a good idea to put Winnie in the crosshairs? You know I have your back, man, but this is a lot, even for you. Do you honestly think Alain is going to accept this coup? Just take it in stride and hand things over to you without a fight? What if shit goes off the rails—what then?"

"No one is going to fuck with me. No one is going to fuck with Winnie, she's mine. She always has been, and she always will be." I will lay down my life for her, protect her instead of walking away like I did years ago.

Then, she was too young, still a child.

Now, she's mine.

I stride to the door, leaving Teague to keep an eye on things from here. When I reach the door, I eye him over my shoulder. "I'm taking Winnie home now. And I need you to handle whatever bullshit comes to our door."

There is not a thing in the world that is going to keep me from my honeybee tonight.

Chapter 21

Debauchery

Winnie

Humiliation battles with fear and anger.

I stood. Teetered across the stage on heels so high I was in another atmosphere. Spun around, making sure the room full of foul and disgusting human beings could see me from every angle. It was only fair they got a good look at the merchandise before shelling out an ungodly amount of money.

Hell, I'm half-shocked no one demanded my virginity to be certified by a trusted expert. Truth in advertising and all that.

One by one, the other girls who were sold off tonight disappear from the dressing room behind the stage. Security corralled us here immediately after the bidding ended and the mountain of a man standing outside the door seems to be serious about making sure we stay safe and secure. The irony isn't lost on me.

More than half the girls have been claimed when the low buzz of conversation filters through the door. The volume grows, voices growing gruff and angry as they approach.

"You do not want to test me. She's mine and I'm taking her now." Christophe shoves through the door and the room is filled with...him. His broad shoulders, piercing blue eyes, and singular focus are directed straight at me. In a huff, he pulls the suit jacket from his body and wraps it around me, enveloping me in his scent, his warmth.

"What are you doing?" I push at the fine wool of his coat, sloughing it off my shoulders only for him to pull it back into place.

"Keep that on"—he grasps the lapels, holding them tightly together as he guides me toward the door—"and move. We don't have much time."

I make a desperate grab at the detached skirt that makes up the rest of my dress. The crimson silk catches on the door, shredding as Christophe pushes me through. I cringe. The gorgeous fabric is in tatters—not that I'll ever wear this ensemble again. I'm sure there's no need for formal wear in my future.

Christophe ushers me out the back of the club and into his waiting car. The driver closes us in and then peels away as one of the suited men from the auction comes barreling out of the building, yelling, threatening. He pulls a weapon from his coat, aiming, trailing the car until we turn the corner and disappear.

"What are you doing?" I ask, spinning to look behind us. "Where are you taking me?"

"Home." His answer is simple, tone entirely too unaffected for the situation.

"What? Why?" I perch on the edge of the plush leather seat to stare at him, but he gives me nothing. All I have is Christophe's stern profile as he calmly taps at his phone. "Someone bought me, paid a fuck of a lot of money for the privilege of debauching me. You can't just steal me away, dammit."

"I can and I did."

My mouth falls open at his curt response. "But the debt; I owed you."

"You still do."

Shock paints my face. "I have no way to pay you back, Christophe. That's what you've told me—insisted on—all along. You almost ruined me in the office before that shit show even started and now...what? You're going to steal me away and try to sell me again? Didn't bring in what you thought you would the first time?" God, I'm pissed—so fucking mad. At him. At my parents. At this whole fucked up situation.

This time, I get nothing in response.

Nothing verbal.

No. Christophe just leans back into the supple leather seat and spreads his knees wide.

"You can start anytime," he says, tilting his head to the space between his feet. His implication is clear.

How many times has he told me I couldn't work off the stupid debt? How many times has he told me the number was too high, the interest too steep?

"You said—"

"Get on your knees or don't, Winifred. We can wait if you prefer, but money has been transferred. Your sale is finalized, and I assure you, the spoils have been claimed and the owner will get his due." A muscle in his jaw jumps, but his eyes are heavy with lust and desire.

"What did you do?"

Finally—*finally*—he meets my eyes, and his lips pull up on the side, his smirk full of threats and promises.

"You can't. You...you didn't *buy* me. You weren't even out there." My voice is high, squeaky. It sounds foreign to me, and full of panic. Though, rightfully so, because I am fucking panicking.

The car stops outside his mansion and the driver

opens the door, his expression grim and weirdly pissed off.

As Christophe steps elegantly from the car, I scramble for the opposite door, but his strong hands stop my escape and pull me back.

"Let me go, you asshole." I twist and try to pull free, but it's useless. My arms are trapped within the steel band of his. He palms my throat, his fingers pressing in.

He spins me, releasing the hold he has on my body, but he doesn't give me my freedom. No, he backs me into the cold metal of the car, pinning me there.

My pulse flutters under his fingertips and like he can't resist the thrill, he tightens his grasp, squeezing, cutting off my air.

"You bastard," I rasp. It's sexy as fuck to feel that vibration against the palm of his hand.

My nipples tighten to hard buds despite myself. I fight, push at him, scratching at his hand and drawing blood. But I get nowhere.

"This little show of defiance is cute, Winnie. I like your fire. But I will not tolerate this shit." His gaze flicks to the crimson droplets blooming at the edge of his stark white dress shirt. "And I think we're done with you making me bleed, do you understand me? It's my turn, now." Furious, he's fucking furious.

Maybe he expects me to cower. To show fear or at

the very least a little respect, but he's obviously wasted his precious time, because *Defiant* could quite literally be my middle name.

"You like that, *chère?*" He squeezes his fingers, and the edges of my vision start to fade.

My grip on his wrists slackens and I feel myself fading. My bravado slipping away along with my grasp on the here and now.

"That's better. Save your energy, honeybee. You're going to need it."

Christophe dips low and tosses me over his shoulder carrying me into his house. The last thing I see before the door closes behind us, are the taillights of the town car fading in the distance as it roars down the driveway.

His firm grip on my thigh keeps me in place as he bounds up the stairs. How he manages to scale them— two at a time—all while stroking his thumb across my center is beyond me.

He turns and stalks down the hallway, entering a huge suite that's got to take up the full wing above mine, slamming the door shut behind us. He shifts and in slow motion I slide down his body feeling every perfectly formed dip and bulge along the way. *The bulge.*

Seconds tick by and he simply holds me in place. Staring. Breathing us in.

My muscles tighten, desire coiling deep in my belly

as I tell myself my reactions are *not* okay. Because while I should be fighting for my life, trembling in fear. My wet panties are proof that something else is making me tremble.

Minutes pass and I shift my weight, pressing my thighs together desperate for friction. I drop my gaze to his mouth; his lips are plump and perfectly still. Not a twitch. Nothing.

Hours.

Years.

A lifetime passes before his mouth crashes against mine. With my hands against his chest, I push at him. Not because I want to, but because I *should*. Everything about this screams at me to resist.

I don't stand a chance.

He presses me to the wall, his body flush against mine from our knees to our hips, our chests to our lips. And while he towers over me, even in these ridiculously high stilettos, there is nothing but packed planes of solid muscle beneath my palms. When he pushes his hips in close, I can't help but gasp.

He licks into my mouth as he thrusts his cock, hot and hard, against my belly. He kisses me stupid. Devours me. Makes me want to give in and work off my parents' debt—by pennies, not dollars.

When I'm good and breathless, and obviously

suffering the effects of oxygen deprivation, he pulls back just enough to grumble, "Now, get rid of this." He slides a thick, blunt finger under the silk band strategically wrapped around my chest.

Broad shoulders bunch and shift as he works his tie loose, carefully folding the bloodred silk and tossing it to the back of his sofa.

"Now, Winnie. Do not keep me waiting."

I side-step him and strut across the room, twisting awkwardly to lower the side zipper that somehow manages to keep this sad excuse of a dress in place. The silk falls from my body leaving me in nothing but my thong and heels as I approach the wall of windows. The view from my room is similar, but with the elevation, the view is so much clearer. The focus displayed much more prominently by the dark wood frames. It's so beautiful, so meaningful that Christophe wanted it perfectly framed.

"Lose the thong." His tone is dark, somewhere between pissed off and lust, but it has the right effect.

I want his hands on me.

I want to feel his touch everywhere.

I hook my thumbs in the scrap of lace and shift my hips sliding the fabric down my body. I kick my panties to the side and shake out my hair, blonde curls spilling down my bare back, and start to toe out of my shoes.

Christophe

"Those stay on," I say, impressed with how steady my voice comes out. Because sweet little Winnie could very well bring me to my knees with that fucking body.

I tried to resist her. I fucking tried to let her go, but there was no way in hell I could do that.

Fuck, the minute I tasted her honey mixed with my whiskey, I knew she had to be mine.

And now, I'm done waiting.

I stalk toward her and take her mouth. Our tongues tangle, warring with each other.

She arches into me, tits firmly pressed against my chest, her sweet little nipples hard against me.

I drop to my knees in front of her for the second time tonight and part her pretty pussy, licking deeply, tasting her. I drive my tongue inside, swirl a tight circle around her clit, and then suck on it. *Hard.*

Her gasp turns to moans as her body shudders.

"Give it to me, honeybee. The count starts now," I rasp, unwilling to take my mouth from her. I throw her leg over my shoulder and pull hard, sucking and teasing until she comes apart on my tongue, my name spilling from her lips.

As Winnie gasps for air, I stand. My cock is like steel. I've waited a lifetime for her. I spin her, placing her palms against the plate glass of the window and pull her hips back so she's bent over and on display. Her stilettos lift her pert ass like it's a gift, just for me. Taking my payment in full is going to be a fucking pleasure.

She watches my reflection as I undo my shirt, one button at a time. When it slides from my shoulders, falling to the floor, she takes her bottom lip between her teeth, biting back a moan. Her eyes trace the ink scrawled across my chest, taking in the story written in images. The moment she lands on the honeybee inked over my heart; she stills.

"Christophe."

Now is not the time. I swat her ass, appreciating the ripple that goes through the plump cheek. Her skin pinks beautifully, leaving behind a perfect handprint.

"Brace," I growl as my cock springs free from my trousers. I grip the base and drop my free hand to the center of her back, positioning her where I want her. I notch my dick at her opening and find her eyes in our reflection.

Ironically, I'm the one who needs to brace because if I don't hold myself back, I'm liable to fuck her through the window. And as much as I talk a big game, I don't want to hurt her.

This is her first time. She's tight and with my size, it's

going to be uncomfortable for her. If I'm rough, I'll split her in two.

If I hurt Winnie, I won't be able to have her again tonight and I don't want to wait. I want to lose myself in her tight heat, make her moan, and hear my name on her lips as she floods my dick.

If nothing else, I'm a goddamn gentleman when it comes to buying virgins and fucking them.

Except, I've never done this.

Never bought a woman—never had to—and sure as fuck have never taken a virgin. Never had any desire for that—not until I found my honeybee again.

I take a deep breath and ease myself forward, and before I breach her opening, she moves.

Instead of bracing, instead of doing as I told her, Winnie rocks her hips, impaling herself on me.

And the one screaming out a name, is me.

Chapter 22

D.T.F

Winnie

Wild.

Unrestrained.

Completely out of control. That's how Christophe fucks me.

I held my breath at the feel of his broad head notched at my center. I waited, anticipating the inevitable pain that's synonymous with losing one's virginity.

But really, it was excitement. The promise of being stretched and filled. The promise of being fucked.

Our gazes were locked in the dark reflection of the window. Indecision? Caution?—I don't know. Something flashed across his face, and he didn't move.

I waited, fully expecting, wanting him to twist his fist in my hair and slam home. Rid me of the stupid label that made men with way too much money lose their fucking minds.

But he didn't.

He paused. Stilled.

Hesitated

So I took matters in hand. I blew out the air I'd held in my lungs for far too long and pushed my hips back, spearing myself on his dick.

Stars flashed behind my eyes at the feeling of fullness.

Obviously, I have no comparison, but Christophe is *big*.

I don't feel a pinch. It's not a hint or a bite of pain. It's a damn life changing intrusion that threatens to split me wide open and spill an ocean of tears.

But I'm not alone in this.

Christophe's fingers dig into my hip as his free hand slides up the center of my back, finally twisting in my hair, the bite at my scalp distracting from the feeling of being torn apart.

His hips are flush against my ass and I'm grateful for the moment to catch my breath. Because the minute he says my name, growling it like he's the one having sex for the first time, Christophe fucking moves.

He drags out slowly and then thrusts in hard, slamming into me, fucking me thoroughly; all I can do is hold on and pray that I make it through to the finish.

"Fuck," rolls off his tongue, the tone guttural and primal.

Deft fingers slide from my hip and swirl in tight circles around my clit, teasing the bundle of nerves, coiling the muscles in my core until I explode.

My legs tremble and no matter how hard I try, my fingers find no purchase against the glass.

If Christophe didn't have one arm wrapped around me and the other tangled in my hair, I'd fall to the ground in a puddle of nothingness.

But Christophe pulls free, the loss of him filling me is jarring, and he scoops me into his arms carrying me like his bride.

Not a virginal one though, that's for damn sure.

"That was two. I'm going to need a couple more from you, honeybee." He lays me down in the center of his massive bed and crawls up my body. He curves his big palm around my breast, holding me hostage as he licks, sucks, and feasts on my nipple. He settles between my thighs, filling me in a single thrust.

I gasp, arching my breast into his mouth.

I don't think I can do it. I don't think I'm capable of having another orgasm, my body is spent and sensitive as all hell. "I can't," I whine, hating how breathless I sound.

Christophe laughs, low and dark. "Bullshit. You can and you will." His hips rock, pistoning his cock in and out of me.

My protests morph into moans of pleasure. Squirming away from him becomes rocking and writhing into him, and with absolutely no warning, he pushes me over the edge, and I shatter again.

His breath is hot against my ear. "That's a good girl. I need another," he demands not pausing in the way he plays my body.

Each touch demands pleasure from me, promising even more in return.

Every slide of his body over mine has my insides clenching and my eyes rolling back in my head.

He plants his hands on the mattress and pushes up, shoving his knees hard against the backs of my thighs. Then his hands spread my knees wide.

"Fucking stunning. Jesus, honeybee, you couldn't be any more beautiful. Look at the way your perfect pussy takes my cock. You were made for me." Every delicious word is punctuated with a thrust of his hips.

The change in angle takes my breath away, and this time when I come, Christophe follows me. And it is spectacular.

He throws his head back and buries himself deep inside me. His cock pulses, and I swear I can *feel* his hot cum filling me. And the entire time, his hooded eyes are locked on mine, never straying, his intense focus never wavering.

When he catches his breath, he says, "Fuck yes, honeybee. You are absolutely perfect."

He thrusts lazily, dragging his cock all the way out of me before slowly pushing back in. He watches the movement with nothing short of awe painted across his beautiful face. His lips quirk up on one side pulling a satisfied smirk from him.

"Think you have another in you?" he asks reaching between us and circling my clit with his thumb.

I yelp and try to squeeze my legs closed, but Christophe wedges his body farther between them.

"Stop... Please..." I'm so sensitive, tears spring to my eyes and spill down my cheeks.

His thumb stalls and the torture is almost worse knowing it's there, feeling the featherlight pressure but at the same time, not nearly enough.

I don't want to climax again; I honestly think it would kill me.

Death by orgasm.

That would be a good song title or maybe even the perfect name for a band.

"What's putting that smile on your face, huh?" Christophe continues his leisurely fucking but his thumb? ...Nothing. He holds it perfectly, maddeningly still against my clit.

"You. You're trying to kill me," I whine. I fucking *whine* because that is all I'm capable of at this point.

His chuckle is dark, deep. Filled with promises or maybe it's full of threats that I don't want to think too hard on.

"I'm not trying to kill you, honeybee. I'm filling you full of life."

As his words swirl in the air around us, the reality of what we've done, what I didn't think about when it mattered or pay attention to in the least, washes over me.

We fucked. We fucked hard and took absolutely no precautions. None. Every single muscle in my body goes tight, and I press my palms against the hard planes of his chest.

"What did you do? Holy shit, what did you do?" I swat at him, pushing and writhing to get away. But it's pointless. Nothing I do puts any distance between us, and the more I struggle, the more he laughs. And thrusts.

Before long, I'm moaning my way through another orgasm, Christophe falling over the edge with me.

And then I black the fuck out. Who knew five orgasms could take so much out of me?

I didn't.

I had no idea, because until tonight, I was a goddamn, inexperienced virgin.

I come back to my senses, the few I have, to see Christophe lying on his side, staring at me, his large hand splayed across my stomach.

He doesn't say a word, but a small, satisfied smile pulls at his luscious lips.

"That was—"

"Fucking perfect." He finishes my sentence for me, placing a soft kiss to the spot just above my heart before climbing from the bed.

But that's not what I was going to say.

I shake my head and squeeze my eyes closed. I need a minute to process everything that just happened.

Tears sting and threaten to spill over onto my cheeks. It's too much. All of this, everything...it's just too much.

I don't know who I am anymore.

I don't know anything.

How did I go from trying to escape this life and do the right thing, to this? I literally went from a twenty-two-year-old good girl to being bought and paid for by the French mob. I didn't even know there was such a thing.

Italian? Duh.

Irish? Absolutely.

Russian? Japanese? Yes. I knew those existed, but this? And in this little nothing of a town? No, I had no idea.

And what now? What does the fact that Christophe either bought me at the auction, or stole me from it, mean for me?

I jump, my eyes flying open at the feel of a warm hand on my knee.

Christophe leans over me, a warm washcloth in his free hand. He gently wipes at our combined releases, whispering sweet, sweet words when I flinch at the contact with my sensitive flesh. His tender care just confuses me even more.

"Stop." My voice is small, throaty and unsure.

His hand stills as his gaze tracks an escaped tear sliding down my temple to disappear into my hair. "Winn—"

I shake my head. "It wasn't perfect, it was stupid."

He jerks his head back, obviously offended. He exhales forcefully through his nose and slams the pink-tinged washcloth toward the bathroom.

Anger fights with frustration across his face in an epic battle. "Stupid. You think being with me is stupid." There's no question, he's simply stating it like a fact. "Sorry your first time was such a disappointment, honeybee."

Jesus Christ, men.

I push myself up to sit, wincing slightly as I settle against the headboard, the sheet clutched to my chest.

"The last thing I need to do right now is stroke your ego. It rivals your dick in size, but that's not what I'm saying." I pin him with a withering look, proud of myself for finding my backbone with this man. But I literally have nothing left to lose.

"What the fuck are you saying, then?" He shifts, hands flung out to the sides.

Part of me wants to laugh. Part wants to cry some more. But really, I just need to know what this is. And much as I want answers, I don't know that I want to kick this buzzing beehive.

"Just say it. Ask me whatever you need to so we can go the fuck to sleep." We stare silently at each other until he adds, "I'll pay you. Five grand for your thoughts."

"I thought the saying was a penny for your thoughts?" Why am I fighting him on this?

"Jesus, fuck. Must be a lot of thoughts."

"So many things," I tell him.

Ignoring his scowl, I launch into my list. "You bought me but have been telling me I can't work off this debt. You stormed up here like a caveman, with me flung over your shoulder like a prize and then took the only thing I have of any value. So which is it going to be? Am

I worth something to you? Am I here until I work off what my parents owe you, or are you going to...I don't know, sell me off for what you can? Use me until you're done with me." My voice rises with each word, surprising even me. "What is this, Christophe? What am I?"

I watch as Christophe's mouth opens, closes, and then opens again before he purses his lips and shakes his head. "*Mon bijou.* You are mine, just mine. That is all." His eyes soften and a smile tugs his mouth up into the shadow of a smile. "You always have been, honeybee. I've known it since I followed you home the first time we met to make sure you were safe. I knew it when I found out your father was setting you up with my uncle's men to make drops. With every year I had to stay away, every status report from Teague, every gift I left for you...I knew. Not just that you were mine, but that you owned me in equal measure."

"But..."

He climbs into the bed next to me and pulls me into his arms. "But what?"

I turn to face him, needing to see his reaction when I say this last part. "I'm not on the pill, not on birth control at all. What if—"

He brushes his lips across mine, his tongue licking inside and dancing with my own.

"You're mine, Winn. All of you. Every piece of you, always." He drags me across his body, settling me on his lap so I'm straddling his thick, muscular thighs.

He kisses me until I'm pliant in his arms, needy and aching for him to fill me again.

This time, Christophe enters me slowly. Brings me to climax gently.

And I fall asleep wrapped up in his arms.

Chapter 23

Disaster

Christophe

Voices filter up from the entryway, pulling me from what might be the best sleep I've ever had. I pinch my eyes closed and bury my nose in Winnie's hair, relishing her warm scent, breathing her in.

I want to stay right here, maybe roll her to her back and wake her up with my tongue between her legs. Her moans, the way she gasps my name, are the sweetest sound. I'm sure she's sore, so a kiss would certainly be more welcome than my dick. For now.

No matter how hard I try to shut out the intrusion, the argument drifting up to my suite is growing louder, more demanding. If whoever the fuck is down there with

Teague ends up waking my honeybee, there will be hell to pay.

I ease myself out of the bed, careful not to wake Winnie, and pull on a pair of navy-blue joggers before taking the stairs down to the main level.

It's fucking mayhem.

"What the fuck happened to not disturbing us? You couldn't make a full night," I spit out as my feet hit the cold marble of the entryway. "Who's going to step up and take care of shit when I steal Winnie for our honeymoon? This better be big."

Teague's eyes widen as he blinks back his misplaced surprise. He's a fool if he thinks I'm not going to make that woman my wife and an even bigger fool if he doesn't think I'm going to take her away, show her the world that exists outside the hundreds of acres of woods.

She's never left and it's time she experiences all that there is in the world.

I will absolutely tie her to me, but I'll make sure she never wants for anything.

"I'm sorry, Mr. Robicheaux. This is my fault, but I... you said if I ever needed your help... Sir, it's my mom." Anguish paints the kid's face—teen, really. He's got to be close to sixteen now and his shit show of a mother has been nothing but a drain on him dragging him down with her. Making his life harder than any parent has a right to. Until now, I've been too busy to consider the possibility that she might be even worse than Winnie's parents were.

Feels like a theme. It seems like I'm collecting orphans. But my favorite one is upstairs naked in my bed. All I want is to crawl back between the sheets, wake her up with my tongue, and hear my name on her lips again.

"Where is she, Roux? What'd she do this time?" I ask.

Roux's shoulders shake as he sucks a deep breath into his lungs. His words rush out on the exhale. "She's... she's home now, but it's bad. Her skin is clammy, it's gray. She's fuckin' gray, Mr. R, gray. Her eyes kept rollin' back in her head and I-I-I wasn't sure if she was breathin'. It's bad, sir. Really fuckin' bad. I don't know what to do."

"You call an ambulance?" Teague questions.

Roux whips his head around, eyes wide and trembling from his head to the beat-to-shit soles of his shoes. "I... But... Last time—"

Christ, last time Kanga overdosed, the kid did call 9-1-1 and when the ambulance took his mother away, he was thrown into the system. Nothing like a half wild teenage boy getting slapped into foster care. He was placed with the worst of the worst. I could only imagine the shit that happened to him there.

"Relax. Stay right there," I tell him. "Teague, a word." I tilt my head toward my office.

The minute I'm through the door, I go straight to my auxiliary closet and pull out a crisp white shirt and black suit. I talk as I dress.

"We need to go get her. Call Hibou and let him know we're bringing Kanga in for detox. Have a room prepared for the kid and tell someone to fucking feed him, he looks like he's half starved. His mother obviously hasn't been worried about making sure he's got what he needs." More similarities layer on top of my orphan collection theme.

How many times did I step in for Winnie when she needed something?

When she was hungry and her parents were nowhere to be found.

When her shoes were falling apart, clothes were far too small or threadbare.

I was the one to step in, make shit happen for her. But the motivation there was purely selfish. I wanted to save her from the first time I met her in the woods and as I watched her grow into a woman, I wanted to keep her for my own.

"Will do. And then?"

I shrug my jacket on and turn. "Then we go get the crazy bitch. I'm going to check on Winnie and when we get back, nothing. Not a fucking thing, no interruptions, hear me?"

Maybe he responds, maybe I just don't give a fuck to listen because I push past him and take the stairs two at a time, eager to get to Winnie even if I just have to walk right back out of the room.

It took no time at all for me to get addicted. To her sounds. To her sexiness. To her sweet, sweet honey.

She makes me lose my mind.

On silent feet, I step into my suite. The last thing I want to do is wake her unnecessarily. She needs her sleep to rest up for all the ways I want to take her, love her. Show her that she owns me. I want to mark this girl so the entire fucking world knows she's mine.

Hair stands on the back of my neck as I approach the bed. An icy chill skates down my spine pooling in my gut as dread spreads through me.

She's gone.

My honeybee is fucking gone.

Glass crunches under my shoes as I tear through the rooms—bathroom, sitting room, even the goddamn closet is empty. I hit the switch and bathe my bedroom in the dim glow of lights intended to set a romantic mood or encourage calm. I feel anything but as I take in the rumpled bedding strewn across the floor, and streaks of blood leading out the French doors to the balcony.

She's not just gone, she's been taken.

Someone put their hands on her.

Someone touched her.

Saw her naked body.

And the blood.

Whoever fucking has my woman better be the one bleeding because if they deigned to spill a single drop of hers, the fear she's surely feeling right now, will come back on them ten-fold.

I will burn the fucking world down for her.

"Teague!" My voice echoes down the stairwell all but rattling the windows and setting the light fixtures swinging.

I hit the entryway seconds before Teague enters, hand on his Glock, ready tension rolling off of him. *Good. He's going to need that.* I scan the room for Roux and come up empty.

"Where's the kid?"

"Boss?"

"Where's the fucking kid, T?"

"I don't know; he was right here. What's going on?" He follows me into my office with a quick, fruitless glance into each room on the way.

"Winnie's gone."

"You think she might've tried to leave again? Decided she didn't want this?" He waves his hand around and I briefly consider shooting the fucking thing off his wrist.

"She was taken," I yell, anger fighting for space with the calm I need in order to plan our next move. "The window was smashed and there's sign of struggle." I shed the suit I just donned and grab black tactical gear suiting up as Teague finally follows my lead. "There's a trail of blood."

"Blood? You think the kid had something to do with it?" He pulls open the weapons panel and starts assembling a broad selection of gear and ammunition. "How many?" Teague asks as he pulls his phone from his pocket.

I pick up the lone, out of place paper sitting in the middle of my pristine desk. The message scrawled across it in sloppy, almost childlike writing makes my blood run cold.

I didn't have a choice. They're gonna kill my mom, man. But your girl is at the Parrain's house. Your driver gave you up.

-R

"Call them all in. We need every single one of our

men."

Teague pauses. "All of them?"

"Every last one. Extraction protocol, tactical ready and give them Alain's address. He has her." I go through the motions of checking weapons and strapping up. "I don't care what it takes, we're getting her back. I just got her, finally got my fucking honeybee, I'm not letting go."

"Jesus. And Alain? His men?" My best friend and closest confidant is in go-mode, striding out the door as he waits for final instructions.

"Take them out. Anyone who had a part in this shit gets a fucking bullet to the head. I want pictures, proof of death, whatever." I stride toward the garage, ice in my veins, ready to find my woman and bring her back to me.

"You don't want the honor?" Teague calls after me.

I don't hesitate in my response. "He doesn't deserve honor. Dead is dead and the sooner his black soul has left his body, the better for all of us." Maybe I should feel something—some kind of regret, sadness—since he's been my only family for the past several years, but I can't. Not now when he has Winnie. He took her from me and for that he has to pay.

Teague's gaze meets mine and holds for a beat before he gives me a tight nod. His voice echoes through the house as he moves toward the guest suites. "Garrick!

Mounting up. You're here—get shit ready to receive and triage."

With that, he disappears from my sight, and I take off to find Winnie.

It's been a long time since I've been right with God, but I don't let that hold me back now. Bygones, and all that.

Please God, keep Winnie safe and free of any further harm.

And rain hell on those who have lain hands on her with malice in their hearts.

Chapter 24

Delirious

Winnie

I tried to fight. I did everything I could to keep them from taking me. But I failed. Naked and terrified, I was manhandled through the shattered window by men who were at the auction.

I was pulled from Christophe's bedroom and carried through the woods. Our woods.

I reached out, my fingers grasping for purchase, but all I felt was the rough bark of the gnarled old oak as I was hauled past it.

I tried to scream.

I struggled and tried to break free, but everything went hazy.

The world blurred and went foggy, after I watched them slide a needle into my arm.

I bounced around the cargo area of the SUV they dumped me into, but then...

Everything went dark.

Chapter 25

Disappear

Christophe

We park at the edge of Alain's estate and steal in, slitting throats and taking out everyone in our way.

Teague gives silent direction to my guys, and they spread out, clearing the rest of the rooms, ascending the stairs like the well-coordinated team I pay them to be. And I silently cover the distance to Alain's study—my father's study. Anything of value is always dealt with in the study.

Winnie is fucking valuable.

The only reason we were able to breach the perimeter and take out Alain's security is because I fucking grew up here as much as in my own home. I know this estate better than anyone—the safety measures my father had installed before his untimely death. The escape routes and the kill switches—I know them all. My father was adamant that family—all family —be cherished and protected.

I approach the double doors, my Glock drawn and ready. I, on the other hand, am not prepared for the sight that greets me.

Rivulets of black mascara stain Winnie's face, painting her like a tragic Gothic clown. There are times when a hint of fear in her eyes makes me hard as fuck, but right now I'm irate.

Alain has her perched on his lap; hands cuffed in front of her and terrified. He's doing his level best to appear relaxed, leaning back in his chair, legs wide as if he needs room for a massive set of balls.

He doesn't.

The fucker has Winnie spread open; her legs hooked over his. A slimy smirk pulls at his lips, baring his tobacco-stained teeth like a feral animal.

I want to kill him, rip him from this world and leave him as nothing but a stain of a memory.

"Good of you to visit us," he says as if this isn't going to end with his head separated from his body.

"Let her go."

"Shame on you, Christophe. Never brought sweet Winifred here when you were *les enfants*."

My eyes dart around the room, taking in his sentry to my left, pistol pointed straight at my head. I mark the position of Alain's hand and the gun he has pressed hard under Winnie's chin.

The other hand...

"So sweet. So soft and wet." He groans as that other goddamn hand snakes between her thighs to cup her sex, his middle finger sliding along the seam of her bare pussy. "You should feel this—how wet she is. Fucking dying for my cock." He spreads his fingers and asks, "Can you see her cunt weeping for me?"

Winnie's chest heaves as a silent sob rips through her and my vision goes red.

I push back the mindless fury, banking it for later. Right now, I need to be calm. Calculating.

One step toward them, toward *her*, and Alain slides his finger back into place, rubbing, probing, assaulting her. And on the other hand?—that finger leaves the guard, instead caressing the trigger in a heavy warning.

"Careful, nephew. Wouldn't want anything to happen to this sweet little treat before we get a chance to taste her." Alain scoffs and shakes his head. "Oh, but you've already had a taste, haven't you? Presumptuous little shit, just like your father was. He thought he was better than me, too. Thought he was untouchable. Unreachable."

Teague steps over the threshold, joining me in this nightmare, and draws the aim of the sentry's second gun.

Alain nods in Teague's direction. "Mind your tiger before he pounces and does something rash. Someone could get killed with his kind of carelessness."

It's the smug smile on Alain's face that has me recalculating the risk involved with just fucking shooting him.

The arrogant prick stole into my house, took my woman. He bound her hands and has his all over her. Touching her where only I've touched her.

He made her cry.

He fucking made her bleed.

He's got to die.

"It's simply delicious watching you squirm. Your thoughts are written across your face, plain as day. That's not such a good trait to have in this business...or this family. It's one of the things that got your father killed." Alain shifts and settles his legs farther out to the sides, spreading Winnie open even more. Her soft brown eyes plead with me, begging for me to help her.

"My father was murdered by the Irish mob. Don't embellish the story, your aggrandizement is too much, even for you, Alain."

His body goes rigid at my familiar use of his name.

Anything to throw him off his game, praying the distraction will give me the opening I need.

The whites of his eye are visible all around his black irises as a red flush creeps across his face. Spittle flies as he roars, "You will show me fucking respect, boy. I'm the head of this organization. The head of this family. I sit behind this desk. I'm the one who holds the power now. Alexandre was a soft-hearted fool...making accords with the Italians and then the Irish. What the hell was that? What was he thinking, working with *de salauds*? Made him look weak...made *le milieu* look weak."

There's a moment, a split second where I think I'll have a chance to make a move, but it passes in the blink of an eye and he becomes even more enraged, digging the barrel of his gun harder into Winnie's neck. I want to rip him to shreds with my bare hands. Wrap my hands around his throat and squeeze until I feel the life seep out of him. Instead, I'm listening to him rant, looking for my opportunity.

"I am your *oncle, Parrain—Caïd—*of this family and I demand you give me the respect I'm due. Years of negotiations, promises of allegiance"—he turns his head and spits his disgust to the thick Persian rug—"I brought this family back from the brink of ruin. It took my brilliance, my cunning and my huge set of *couilles* to fix what your father did. The Italians? The fucking Irish? Who aligns with the fucking Irish?"

He sits up straight, shoving his body forward, folding in over Winnie and making her flinch at the ever increasing intrusion.

He needs to die.

"A few well-placed comments that the Italians were getting preferential treatment, more favorable terms, the hint that they were being lured in so they could be taken care of, removed from the equation, and the Irish were more than happy to help clear my way to the top. We didn't even have to get our hands dirty."

Every time he mentions the Irish, Teague stiffens beside me. The distinction, the dismissal, hits with the force Alain intends and the air in the room shifts even darker.

"I thought I could keep you under my thumb, Christo, and I did for a very long time. Gave you the territories no one else wanted, the impossible accounts that no one could get to fall in line—the fucking L'Oursons for Christ's sake. Instead, you took care of their daughter. Gave her money, made sure she had what she needed. You bought her little gifts, leaving them on her doorstep when she needed them—food, clothing—and now, what, you fall for her? I dumped them on you in order to watch you fail. Become further indebted to me.

"But you've very kindly shown me that's no longer a viable option, there's no place in this *famille* for you any more than there was for Alexandre. I rid this world of your father and I will happily dispose of you in similar fashion. All I ask is for one move, a flinch, something to assuage my complicity in your expungement."

I'm shocked.

I'm stuck.

My father's only brother—his only living relative—orchestrated his death. Manipulated organizations, tore down bridges being built in order for all the families in the area to work together.

He killed my father. Ripped him away and deprived me of growing up, maturing, under my father's guidance, leaving me at the mercy of his murderer.

"And *Maman*?" I ask. Even though I know, I need him to confirm that he had my mother slaughtered as well. My sweet innocent mother.

A derisive scoff is my only answer.

Rage electrifies everything within me, making my blood run thick like hot sludge through my veins. Bringing every move, every expression into laser sharp focus. I'm completely powerless yet coming unglued at the same time.

There is no way out of this.

If either Teague or I shoot, Alain's reaction will take Winnie out with him.

I scan the room, looking for any, any hint that one of my men is just out of sight, perfectly positioned to end this.

But even then, without a diversion, any shot will result in disaster.

I can't lose Winnie.

I can't live without her. There's nothing left for me to do but give in—to drop my weapon and pray to a god who hasn't been there for me since the day my uncle had my parents killed that I can somehow find a way through this.

"It was simple, really. And it'll be even simpler to do it again and get you out of the way for—"

Two shots ring out in rapid succession, and I swear I almost shit my pants. The idea of losing Winnie when I've finally gotten her is too much for me to bear. But the series of events do not add up. The window has shattered inward, throwing shards of glass at the desk, spraying the occupants in shimmering, razor sharp slivers.

Red blooms in bright splashes against Winnie's bare skin, little pinpricks of hell.

The lone sentry in the corner is leaking heavily as he slumps motionless against the wall.

And Alain... Staring at his still form has me wishing it had been me who took him out.

Chaos rises from momentary silence.

Utter stillness morphs into pandemonium.

Teague dives through the window, dropping from the balcony as he goes after the shooter, allowing me to focus on Winnie.

Her cheeks shine with trails of tears as she trembles uncontrollably, my uncle's blood splattered across her otherwise flawless skin like a Jackson Pollock.

I holster my weapon and reach down to pull her into my arms. I crush her naked form to me, and relief floods my body as I press her close.

She shivers, her whole being juddering.

I turn to grab a throw blanket from the sofa by the bookshelves to cover her but am pulled up short.

Winnie gasps, a scream of terror bursting from her as her eyes go wide and she's ripped away from my hold.

Alain wraps his bloody hand around Winnie's waist and the air wheezes from him, his lips skewed in a lurid grin as he sneers up at me from his perch. "This belongs to me," he rasps, struggling to get to his feet. He uses Winnie to pull himself upright.

Bastard.

The fucking bastard using her to help himself in anyway is offensive.

Metal glints as they shift, Alain standing unsteadily. The blade of his knife—the one he stole from my father—depresses the creamy unmarked skin at Winnie's ribs.

That knife is sharp. At least it used to be.

My father kept the blade honed and oiled, gleaming and deadly. The scar on my left palm from childhood curiosity serves as proof.

But maybe Alain let that go to shit like he has every-thing else. Everything he's stolen from me. Everything that is rightfully mine.

Just like Winnie.

"Enough, old man. Time for you to let go." I keep my tone calm but make sure there is absolutely no room for misinterpretation.

Alain presses the knife harder against Winnie. A flick of his wrist and a well-placed jab would have her covered once again in crimson. This time blood instead of silk.

The only way I'll allow that to happen is over my dead body.

My uncle chuckles low and sinister. "*Non*. This one is mine. Hands up and step back," he orders, face red and breathing labored.

He was hit, I know he was. The force of the blow knocked him out of his fucking chair, had him sprawled on the floor, motionless.

I raise my hands, palms out, and take a step away, laterally as opposed to actually retreating from them. And when Alain shifts, I see it. A scarlet pool slowly expanding, staining the pearlescent white of his dress shirt to rival the black stain on his soul.

"You will let us pass; don't move a muscle. The girl and I are walking out of here and you're going to let it happen, *comprends?*" He pushes Winnie toward the door, struggling when he has to step over the body of one of his men.

How he thinks he's going anywhere with her is beyond me. He's barely ambulatory.

The restraint it takes not to pounce is immeasurable, but he has the edge of a blade pressed to my girl. A rivulet of blood trails from where the tip digs into her skin as he drags her over the prone body of his man.

Her face is a mask of fear.

I meet her gaze, pupils blown wide, and dip my chin hoping she picks up that I've got her. I let her go once, I'm not letting that happen again. No fucking way.

Reality crashes over Alain when they reach the top of the stairs. There's no feasible way he can maintain his tenuous grasp on control of the situation, and that blink of realization is all I need.

I wrap a hand around Winnie's upper arm and push

her away, wedging myself between her and my uncle and launching him down the staircase.

Chapter 26

Devotion

Winnie

I FALL TO THE FLOOR, NAKED, BLEEDING, TERRIFIED.

Christophe and his uncle tumble down the stairs in a chaotic jumble of limbs and flashing metal, grunting the whole way. When Christophe stands, it's with a loud grunt and a bit of a wobble. He lifts his chin, gaze meeting mine through the iron spindles of the banister.

I stare at him, the bars between us a barrier that needs to either be strengthened or destroyed.

"Come."

That's all he says, and my mind stutters to a halt. The last time he uttered that single word, he was buried deep inside me, pulling ungodly pleasure from me.

Now, there is no physical connection between us, just a full flight of stairs and a dead body.

Hopefully.

"Is he...?" Unable to finish that thought, I let it trail off.

Christophe glances down at his uncle, the hilt of a knife protruding from the man's neck. "In hell, where he belongs. Hopefully bent over and getting fucked by the devil himself as a welcome." He nudges Alain's thigh, getting no response.

Dead. He's dead. The monster is definitively gone.

I pull myself upright, standing on legs made of Jell-o.

"Come to me, honeybee."

One hand on the railing, two steps to the top of the stairs, three deep, bracing breaths and I'm there—ready to take my first steps toward salvation.

Willing, not forced.

Drawn, not repulsed.

I begin my descent, slowly. Carefully. Pausing when I hear in a low, sexy growl, "Christ, look at you. Regal like the queen you are. Fucking perfect."

Christophe ascends the stairs, taking them two at a time, as if he can't stand to be away from me any longer. He wraps his hands around me, fingers twisting through my hair, gently guiding my jaw to where he wants me. His lips hover a breath from mine before softly sliding over them. This kiss is different, deliberate, sensual. Reverent.

As it slows, he pulls back, and retreats a step. His hands glide across my shoulders and down my arms until my hands are clasped in his. He holds them out to the side and stares.

I can almost feel each spot as his gaze traces over me, my heavy breasts, the dip of my waist, the flare of my hips. His attention intently focused.

"And I might just have to fire my house staff." The corner of his mouth lifts slightly.

I know I've been through some shit in my life, things that have made absolutely no sense whatsoever, but I can't begin to make sense of his statement.

I shake my head. "Why?"

"Because, honeybee, I want to watch you walk down my stairs just like this. Every day that I'm alive, I want to see you descend from your pedestal on high to grace me with your beauty. Allowing me to bask in every flawless inch of you." His eyes are hooded and full of heat. "But I will kill anyone—fucking anyone—who dares to lay their eyes on what's mine."

In one swift movement, he swoops me into his arms and carries me down to the entryway, carefully stepping over the lifeless body sprawled there. With a purposeful stride, Christophe brings us deeper into the house stopping in a grand living area. He shifts me in his grasp and whips a fresh throw from the back of a tufted leather Chesterfield and wraps it around me, shielding my nakedness.

I meet his gaze expecting to find his smirk, that tilt of his lush lips, only to see a hard scowl. I flinch.

Christophe sets me on my feet, adjusts the throw more tightly around me and then scoops me into his arms once again. "I love Teague like a brother; I don't want him to be the first one I have to kill for seeing you bare." And then, I get the smirk that sends my heart racing and makes my thighs clench.

He must feel the tightness of anticipation in my body, because his casual attitude shifts to urgency as his long legs eat up the distance to the car out front. He climbs into the back seat with me still clutched in his arms and directs one of his men to get us home immediately.

Home.

All my life, that word has stood for nothing but stress, anxiety, and shame. Until the very first day I met Christophe in the woods, then he became synonymous with home.

He was my safe haven that summer. He became my silent savior through the years, making sure I had what I needed in life. And now?

His intense stare bores deep into my soul dispatching the illusion that I'll ever be able to withhold anything from him again.

"You are mine, Winnie. Not because you're bought and paid for, though I would do that again in a heartbeat. That was nothing more than a technicality. Your soul speaks to mine. You ground me. You are my reason for being."

I blink back tears at the sincerity of his tone. His words penetrate through the layers of armor surrounding my heart. The only other person to ever make it through that armor is Tru, but this is entirely different, and I can't help but melt as his declarations continue.

"And I plan on spending the rest of my life loving you. Spoiling you. I don't ever want you to go without or want for anything. Nothing is out of your reach, honeybee. Nothing. The world is yours for the taking." He brushes his lips across mine, sealing his proclamation with a kiss. Pulling back, he wraps his fist in my hair giving it a sharp tug and adds, "And I'm going to fuck you, honeybee. Make no mistake, you are mine in every fucking way. I will lay the world at your feet, I will slay all of your dragons, and keep you sheltered, surrounded by the safety of our woods, but I will thoroughly fuck you at every opportunity."

The car rolls to a stop in the circle drive outside his

mansion and before the driver even shifts into park, Christophe hits the intercom button.

"Sit tight until we're inside and then go back for Teague."

The response sounds distant despite the fact that the only thing separating us is an opaque privacy panel. "Sir, it's not a problem to get the door for you."

Christophe's voice is laced with threats and spilling over with venom. "Move a fucking muscle and I will end you, *oui?*"

"Yes, sir."

He climbs out of the car and mounts the steps to the front door, clutching me to his massive frame. "No one gets to see what's mine, honeybee. Never again."

His commitment to that statement is only solidified as he stalks through his entryway, barking threats to anyone who dares to greet the lord of this manor.

He eats up the distance to his suite, shoulders back, expression fierce.

I should be scared.

I should be terrified.

Instead, for the first time ever, I feel safe.

I feel cared for and cherished.

Treasured.

Maybe even loved. I don't know. That might just be too much to ask for in my life.

The door to his suite slams behind us closing us away from the house—from the rest of the world—and Christophe sets me down in the middle of the room.

"What happens now?" I ask.

Right or wrong, I care about him. I always have and I don't think I can survive anything less than full reciprocity.

Christophe stares at me, his full lips pursed, making them even fuller. More alluring. More tempting.

I want to press up onto my toes and taste them, but as I shift my weight, his hold on my shoulders tightens. Not pushing me away, but certainly not pulling me close.

Despite his words and declarations, doubt starts to creep in. Christophe runs hot and fierce, but a chill from his lack of response burrows under my skin, making me jittery and uncomfortable.

I care too much—about him, about his wants and desires. I squirm, trying to pull away from him but, once again, I get nowhere.

"Be still, honeybee." Christophe leans close, his lips barely moving as he pushes the words from his mouth. "You want to know what happens next? This is where we start. Where we reclaim what's been taken from us. This is the start of us, you and me. The start of our empire."

He walks us farther into the room. The bloodied cashmere throw slides from my shoulders as we move, leaving me completely exposed as he presses me close. His warm, solid body is a beacon, a safe haven against the frigid night air swirling through the broken glass door. His tongue swipes across his lower lip, wetting it before he pulls it between his teeth.

He spins me around to gaze out over his grounds, his mouth brushing against my ear as he says, "This is the beginning of our adventure, *ma chère*. The start of our forever. We're going to take back what's rightfully ours and rule over the Robicheaux empire. Bring it back to the vision my father had for it, and then make it even better. Make it completely ours." He kisses a path down my neck and across my shoulder, goose bumps amplified by the warmth of his mouth.

He leads me to the bathroom, shedding his weapons and peeling off his clothes as the water heats. We step into the shower, the water tinted pink with the blood painted over my skin as it swirls around the drain, taking the marks of a horrid man with it.

We take our time lathering our hands and washing each other clean.

Touching.

Caressing.

The temperature rises, though it has nothing to do

with the steamy water and everything to do with the man in front of me.

"You'll always be my honeybee"—he turns us, backing me into the corner and wraps both my wrists in one of his big hands, pinning them against the tile above my head—"but to everyone else, you'll be the queen bee. And I'll spend the rest of my life serving you."

Christophe takes my mouth, devouring me, making me his over and over again, all while declaring that he is mine.

Epilogue

... Dreams

Tru

I did it. I pulled the trigger and now he's dead. Gone forever.

I'm finally safe, at least from him.

The devil no longer has a hold on me. He is no more.

I slide to the ground, the cold and wet soaking through my lounge pants.

The gun falls from my hand, and I expect to feel... free. Completely free.

But since the day I first met Alain Robicheaux, anxiety has been my constant companion.

Even his death—at my own hand, no less—hasn't brought me peace.

No. The only hint of peace I've felt since that godawful day is what I've found in the depths of sharp brown eyes. His voice a melodic balm to my constantly frayed nerves. His touch is the only one I can tolerate. No. I don't just tolerate his touch, I crave it.

The world around me buzzes in a static, disconnected way. And then everything goes still, calm.

Peace rains down on me, swirling like a fog, and wrapping me up in a protective bubble.

The buzz becomes a hum.

The hum becomes a murmur.

The murmur clarifies into words.

But it's all a trick, a figment of my imagination.

"Truie, come back to me. Don't drift away, *a cuisle.* Look at me, come on. I need you here with me."

That voice.

It's the one from my dreams.

...The End?

Thank you for reading this dark reimagining of Winnie the Pooh or, in French, Winnie L'Ourson. Tru

Cochonette (Piglet) and Teague Grey (Tigger) still have their story to tell. The best place to stay in the know on what's going down with them is *here*.

Playlist

Find the complete playlist for Into the Woods on Spotify.

- A GOOD DAY TO D13 - Arankai
- Out of the Woods - Taylor Swift
- Sinner - Of Virtue
- Oxytocin - Chandler Leighton
- Haunting Me - Loveless
- Bully - KAMAARA
- GODLESS - LaLion
- ENDLESS LOVE - Poe the Passenger
- Obsessed - Jules
- The Wikked - Witchz
- Into Those Woods - Bragolin

- The Price Of Power - Crimson, Arankai, Villainous
- MATCH MADE IN HELL - Dutch Melrose, benny mayne

Huge thanks to Amanda for saving me from having to rely on flawed translations from the internet!

Thanks always to Stacy, who read it along every step of the way and gave me so much encouragement and so many good suggestions...and she created this gorgeous cover...Thank you! And to my girls. Without you, I would be so damn lost. I love you!

And of course, my family. I couldn't do this without you. All my love!

Acknowledgments

This was supposed to be a fun, two-week diversion. A little something different to clear my brain: quick, dirty, and totally not my norm. It's been well over a year since I started it and it has grown into something I'm so proud of, as well as something that makes me blush the most deliciously decadent red. So, to Bryce, Morgan, and Kelly, who all thought this was the greatest idea ever... I still love you all, but this was a rough ride!

Add to that the fact that I did a bit of an experiment with this one, and handed out exclusive pre-published copies that contained a special link to a survey. Of the hundred I gifted, four people responded. Four. Reading their thoughts, the things they liked, loved, and wanted more of was amazing. A lot of their insights were taken into consideration when expanding the original novella to the novel it is now. So a special thank you to Marie, Nikki, Ellie, and Violet—without your interest this would have never grown into what it is now!

Also by KC Enders

Troubles

Twist

Tombstones

Beekman Hills: the series

In Tune

Off Bass

Beat Down

Out Loud (coming soon)

Tattered Hearts

Sweet on You

About the Author

KC Enders thrives on strong coffee, good bourbon, and the anguished tears of unsuspecting readers. Every now and then, she sprinkles in a good laugh to balance out the shredding of hearts.

To laugh, cry, and curse her name, dive into her other titles. *The most current information can be found on her website.*

She loves talking books, hearing from readers, and hosting the occasional virtual Happy Hour in her reading group.

facebook.com/kcewrites

instagram.com/authorkcenders

bookbub.com/profile/kc-enders

tiktok.com/@kcenderswrites